Other books by Leah Williamson

You Have the Power

Written with Suzanne Wrack

The Wonder Team
and the Forgotten Footballers

Written with Jordan Glover

The Wonder Team
and the Pharaoh's Fortune

Written with Jordan Glover

The Wonder Team
and the Rainforest Rescue

Written with Jordan Glover

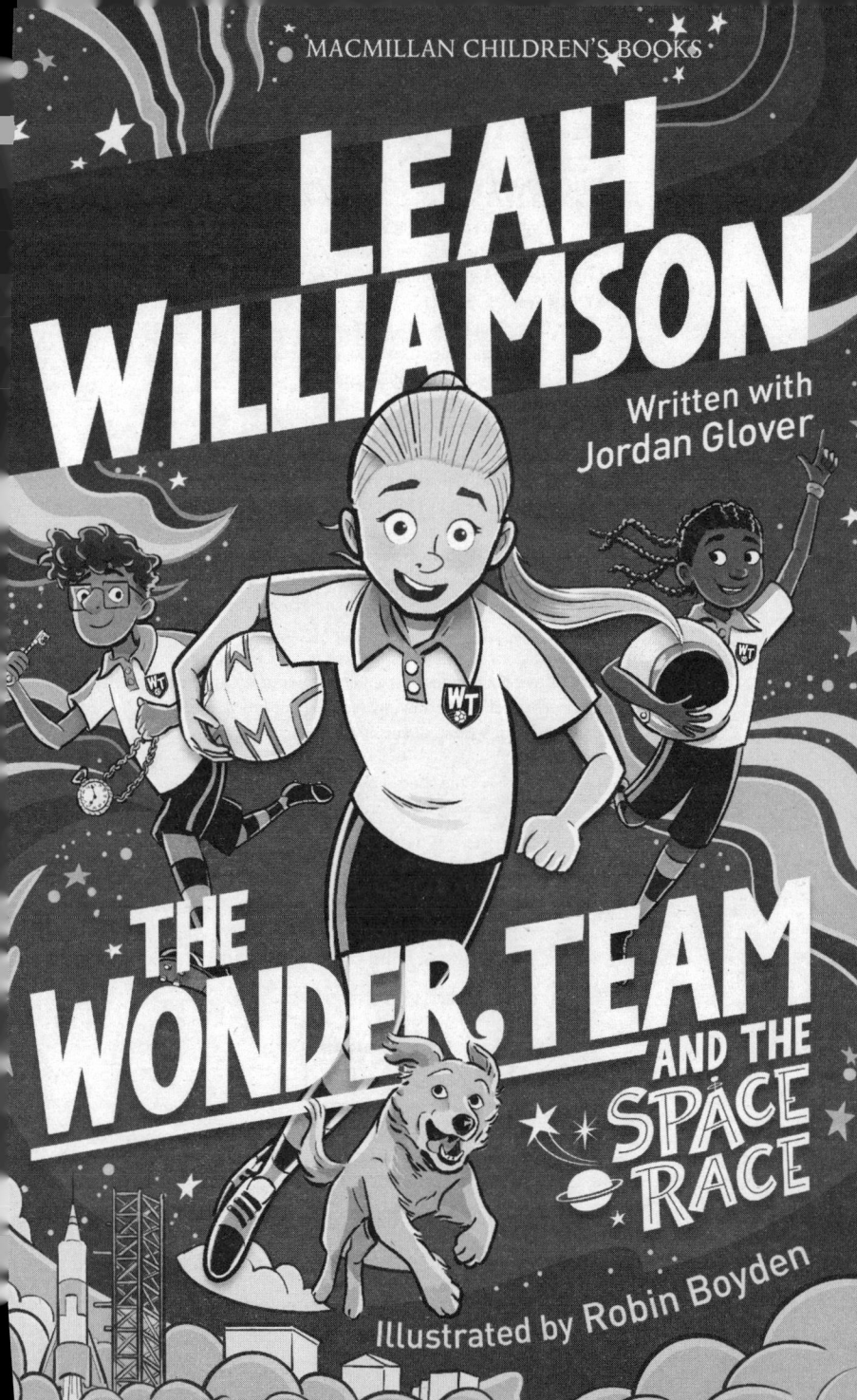

Published 2025 by Macmillan Children's Books,
an imprint of Pan Macmillan
The Smithson, 6 Briset Street, London EC1M 5NR
EU representative: Macmillan Publishers Ireland Ltd, 1st Floor,
The Liffey Trust Centre, 117–126 Sheriff Street Upper
Dublin 1, D01 YC43
Associated companies throughout the world
www.panmacmillan.com

ISBN 978-1-0350-5480-0

Text copyright © Leah Williamson and Jordan Glover 2025
Illustrations copyright © Robin Boyden 2025

The right of Leah Williamson, Jordan Glover and Robin Boyden to be
identified as the authors and illustrator of this work has been asserted by them
in accordance with the Copyright, Designs and Patents Act 1988.

All rights reserved. No part of this publication may be reproduced,
stored in a retrieval system, or transmitted, in any form or by any means
(electronic, mechanical, photocopying, recording or otherwise),
without the prior written permission of the publisher.

Pan Macmillan does not have any control over, or any responsibility for,
any author or third-party websites referred to in or on this book.

1 3 5 7 9 8 6 4 2

A CIP catalogue record for this book is available from the British Library.

Printed and bound by CPI Group (UK) Ltd, Croydon CR0 4YY

This book is sold subject to the condition that it shall not, by way of trade or otherwise,
be lent, resold, hired out, or otherwise circulated without the publisher's prior consent in
any form of binding or cover other than that in which it is published and without a similar
condition including this condition being imposed on the subsequent purchaser.

To our mums and our dads. We never would have got to where we are now without the love, support, and guidance you've given us over the years. We'll always be grateful.

CHAPTER 1: THE TWANG

Leah groaned in frustration as she watched the ball soar over the hands of the Crickle End goalkeeper. It hit the back of the net with a triumphant *thwack*. The whistle sounded. Opposite Leah, Ayo, the other defender, shook her head in defeat.

That was the *third* goal their opponents had scored. Crickle End High hadn't even come close to scoring one and there was only a quarter of the match left.

'Come on, guys!' Miss Kaur shouted from the sideline as the team trudged back to their starting positions. 'Don't give up. We've still got time to turn this around!'

Leah wasn't so sure. They'd known that the team from Thornton Brook were good and they'd expected a challenge, but she hadn't thought it would be *this* difficult.

The weather wasn't making things any easier. Rain fell over the pitch in a light mist. Their kits were soaked through, and the tips of Leah's fingers were starting to go numb. She rubbed her hands together, but it did nothing to banish the chill.

'This is torture,' Mimi groaned, jogging over to Leah's side.

'I don't understand how they keep scoring,' complained William, as he and Ayo joined them.

Ayo scrunched up her nose. 'Their strikers are just too fast,' she said.

'We can't keep up with them,' Leah agreed. She scowled at the opposing team.

'We're doing the best we can,' Mimi said, placing a comforting hand on Ayo's shoulder. 'It's no one's fault.'

Leah bit her lip, averting her eyes. Mimi might not be placing blame, but Leah couldn't help but feel responsible. It was her job to defend the goal, and so far she'd failed spectacularly. She had to do *something* to stop Thornton Brook's imminent victory.

The four of them split up, jogging over to take their places. The whistle blew and Leah bounced on her toes. If they were going to turn the tide of this match, she had to *focus*.

The midfielder from Thornton Brook had the ball, and he sped down the pitch towards Leah, leaving the Crickle End High players trailing behind him. Ayo rushed forward to meet him, her feet dancing across the wet grass as she attempted to intercept the ball. But, just like before, the Thornton Brook player was faster, and he dodged and weaved around her, edging closer to the goal.

Leah felt adrenaline burn up inside her. There was *no way* she could let them score again.

She surged towards the midfielder. He was already preparing to pass the ball, but Leah was ready for him. She jerked to the side, cutting him off and forcing him to turn the ball in a clumsy circle. She saw an opening. It was tight, and a little bit risky, but Leah didn't stop to think about it. She lunged forward, her foot hooking around the ball and dragging it away from the midfielder.

'Yes!' she yelled, a wild grin on her face.

And then a searing pain shot up her leg.

Her triumphant cry turned into a strangled yelp as her knee gave way, sending her crashing to the grass. It was like something inside her leg had snapped. The ball spun away from her, but Leah didn't care as she gripped her knee, gasping. Her entire leg burned. She squeezed her eyes shut, breathing fast.

Vaguely she heard the whistle blow, and then there were people crowding around her.

'L, are you okay?' Mimi said anxiously.

'What happened?' George asked. He'd sprinted over from the sideline when he'd seen Leah go down.

Leah groaned in response.

'Her face has gone totally white, miss.'

'Thanks, William, I can see that,' came Miss Kaur's voice, and then Leah felt a hand on her arm. 'Leah, can you tell me where it hurts?'

'My knee,' Leah managed to gasp. 'There was

a twang and it just . . . went.'

'Oh dear,' Miss Kaur said, her voice full of worry. 'You must have pulled something. You'll have to come off.'

Leah pushed herself up onto her elbows. 'Miss—'

But the coach's voice was firm. 'Leah, you can't play if you can't run. You need to let your knee rest.'

Disappointment welled up inside Leah. She knew Miss Kaur was right, but that didn't make it any easier.

With Miss Kaur's help, Leah hobbled over to the sideline. She gritted her teeth against the pain throbbing through her knee.

'Here,' Miss Kaur said, directing her over to the bench. 'Sit down and keep your leg elevated. I'll send someone to get you an ice pack.'

Miserably, Leah did as she was told. George handed her a coat, and she pulled it on, putting up the hood to protect against the rain. On the pitch, the game restarted. Leah watched, her entire body itching to be out there with her teammates. She glared at her throbbing knee. She'd never had an injury like this before; she hoped the pain would fade soon and that it wouldn't keep her benched for long.

But . . . what if it did?

Fear wormed through her as she thought about the professional footballers she admired. Some of them had suffered injuries that had stopped them from playing for *months* at a time.

Why had she made that tackle? She'd known it was a risky move, but all she'd been thinking about was stopping the Thornton Brook player from scoring.

Leah turned her attention to the match and tried not to worry about the burning pain in her knee. It probably wasn't anything to worry about, she told herself. She'd be back playing next week. She was sure of it.

But by the time the match had finished and the defeated Crickle End High players trudged to the changing room, Leah's knee was still throbbing painfully, and suddenly she wasn't very sure at all.

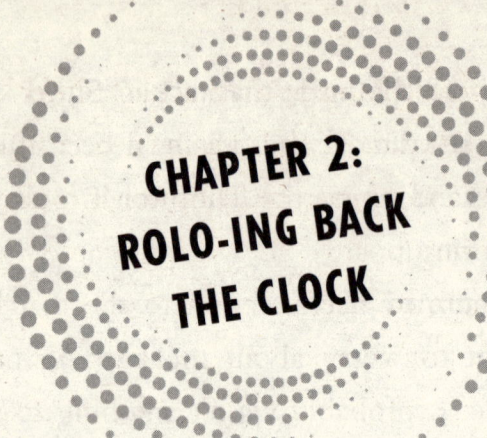

CHAPTER 2: ROLO-ING BACK THE CLOCK

When Mimi and George poked their heads around the door of Leah's bedroom that weekend, she was lying in bed, reading a book. She smiled at the sight of her friends and put it down.

'I'm so happy to see you,' Leah gushed as they came inside. Both of them were wearing jeans and hoodies, and behind them a familiar brown-and-white dog burst into the bedroom. It gave a happy *woof* and jumped up onto Leah's bed, licking her face enthusiastically. 'Rolo!'

'I thought he might cheer you up,' Mimi said. 'Your mum said you were feeling a bit fed up.'

'Is that all she said?' Leah muttered grumpily. 'I'm surprised she didn't tell you not to get me overexcited.'

George and Mimi looked at each other.

'She did, didn't she?' Leah cried. She closed her eyes and let her head tip back against her wooden headboard. 'She's a nightmare. I'm not *ill*, I've hurt my knee!'

'She's just worried about you,' Mimi said gently.

'Anyway, she wasn't *only* talking about you,' George added. 'She also said she'd bring us some lunch soon. It's nearly twelve.'

'I bet it's soup,' Leah huffed. 'That's all she's

fed me since we got home from the doctor's yesterday.'

George looked down, fixing his eyes on the cream carpet. 'Yeah, she did say something about lentil soup, actually . . .' He trailed off.

Leah huffed again and stroked Rolo's ears. 'I could probably deal with all of their fussing if I wasn't so bored,' she complained. 'The doctor said I've got to rest and, *of course*, Mum and Dad are being all over the top about it. Dad won't even let me go for a wee without help!'

'Well, he is a nurse,' George pointed out. 'He knows what he's talking about.'

Leah glared at him.

'Does it still hurt?' Mimi asked, pointing towards Leah's knee. It was resting on a cushion, the electric-blue support bandage wrapped around it clearly visible.

'Not any more,' Leah replied. 'I can walk on it like normal. But the doctor told me I can't play football for another two weeks. She said if I do too much exercise, the pain will come back and I might damage my knee forever. I've got to wait for the swelling to go down.'

'Two weeks?' George said, his eyebrows raised. 'That's ages!'

'I know,' Leah said glumly, hugging a squirming Rolo to her chest. 'It sucks.'

'I'm sorry, L.' Mimi patted her hand. 'But if you do what the doctor tells you, you'll be back on the pitch in no time.'

'Which is a good thing, because the team is rubbish without you,' George piped up, smiling mischievously.

'Hey!' Mimi exclaimed. She grabbed a fluffy pillow off Leah's bed and threw it at George.

Leah and Mimi burst out laughing as George threw the pillow back. Rolo launched himself off the bed, bounding around them and filling the bedroom with his high-pitched barks. Leah only laughed harder, and some of the gloom that had been hanging over her since her doctor's appointment started to disappear.

Once the laughter had died away, and as Rolo wandered away to sniff around Leah's desk, Leah sighed. 'I just hope the next two weeks go by quickly,' she said. 'I'm not very good at waiting on the sidelines.'

'We know how much you love football, L.' George's face was serious. 'But you just have to be patient.'

Leah didn't say anything, gritting her teeth in frustration.

Suddenly, Rolo let out a yelp, and Leah leaned forward to see the little dog sitting patiently in front of her bookshelves. He stared at her expectantly.

'What's up, boy?' Mimi asked, crouching next to him. She ran her hands over his silky coat.

Rolo barked again. Then he jumped up, resting his paws on one of the lower shelves. He nudged his nose against a silver metal box.

It was the box that Leah and her friends had found beneath a great, upturned oak tree in the park. Back then, it had only contained an old-fashioned pocket watch with a mysterious inscription on the back. But the watch did so much more than tell the time.

It had the ability to send them back into the past. With the watch's power, Leah, Mimi and

George had been on a number of time-twisting adventures. Most recently to the Tanzanian rainforests in 1968, where they'd rescued a troop of chimpanzees from the clutches of a sinister poaching group. Even now, Leah couldn't help but shudder as she remembered the way the leader of the poachers had sneered as he'd threatened Mwamba, a baby chimpanzee.

But since they'd returned, the watch had stayed inside the box, alongside three other magical objects that had gradually appeared after each of their adventures – a compass, a magnifying glass and, most recently, a key. It wasn't that Leah and her friends hadn't *wanted* to go back in time again, but they'd learned that the watch never worked when they wanted it to. It always seemed to have a plan of its own.

Rolo barked again, dragging Leah from her thoughts. She smiled and shook her head. 'I don't think there'll be any adventures for me until my knee has healed up, boy,' she said.

'I wonder where the watch'll take us next,' Mimi pondered.

'Nowhere good, probably,' said George with a frown. 'Definitely somewhere with snakes. We *always* end up somewhere with snakes.'

'We never actually saw a snake in Tanzania, though,' Leah pointed out.

George scoffed. 'We were too busy with the dangerous poachers, enormous landslides and wild leopards!'

'At least the baby chimpanzees were cute,' Mimi offered with a weak smile.

Rolo barked again and Leah frowned. 'Come on, Rolo, cut it out.'

But rather than backing away, Rolo jumped upwards, butting his head so hard against the side of the box that it went crashing down to the floor. The lid popped open and the contents fell out. Leah lurched up from the bed with a gasp, careful not to agitate her knee.

'Rolo!' Mimi scolded. 'Look what you've done now!' She leaned down, picking up the magnifying glass, whilst George collected the key, which had landed near his foot. Leah grabbed the compass, but then she froze. *Where was the watch?* She scanned the floor, desperately searching for the silver glint of its casing.

Rolo barked once more, but this time, the sound was muffled. It was as though something were stopping the sound.

Leah gasped.

The watch was in Rolo's mouth!

Without thinking, Leah lunged forward, reaching for the silver chain hanging out from between the spaniel's teeth. She hooked it on her little finger just as Rolo tried to scamper away.

'No, Rolo!' Mimi was shouting. 'Drop it!'

'Oh no,' George muttered, his hands twisting nervously together. 'Don't pull too hard, L. What if it breaks?'

'Come on, Rolo!' she muttered through gritted teeth. 'Let . . . go!'

And, suddenly, Rolo did as he was told – the watch popped free. Caught by surprise, Leah stumbled backwards, her feet tripping clumsily over the carpet. A sharp flare of pain in her knee made her gasp and she felt her leg buckle as she crashed backwards into her friends.

Instinctively, Leah clutched the watch.

As she did so, her finger pushed against the little gold crown at the top of its casing. She felt it click twice. Her eyes flicked towards the clock mounted on the wall above her bed.

She already knew what it was going to say.

Twelve o'clock. Noon.

Leah's stomach swooped as the familiar walls of her bedroom disintegrated into a twisting mass, the colours swirling together like oil and water. She squeezed her eyes shut, trying to ignore the twingeing pain in her knee as she, Mimi and George were catapulted into the tangled threads of the past.

CHAPTER 3: THE CRASH

When the world stopped spinning, Leah found herself in darkness.

'Ugh!' came Mimi's voice from the left. 'I can't see anything!'

'*Ah!*' squealed George. 'Something furry just touched me!'

'Hang on, hang on!' Trying to ignore how fast her heart was beating, Leah stumbled forward, her hands outstretched. They met a cool surface, and she groped along it until she felt something familiar. A handle! She pushed down.

The door swung open and Leah tripped forwards. Mimi and George were just behind her and the three of them tumbled out of the darkness into a heap on the floor.

'Hey!' came a sharp voice. 'Watch where you're going!'

Leah looked up to see a dark-haired man in a suit staring down at her with a frown. He shook his head in disapproval before stalking away.

'Sorry!' Leah called after him as she scrambled to her feet. Her knee was aching and she winced, rubbing at the blue bandage.

'Oh no, L!' Mimi gasped as she stood. 'Is it your knee?'

Leah shook her head, reaching to help George up. 'No, I'm all right. It was just a twinge.'

Once they were all on their feet, George straightened his glasses and looked around. 'Where are we?'

The last time they'd travelled with the watch, they'd landed in the middle of a rainforest. Although Leah, Mimi and George hadn't known exactly *where* they were, it had been obvious that they were no longer in Crickle End. This time, however, it was much harder to tell. They were in a long corridor, the mushroom-coloured walls stretching away in either direction. Behind them, the door they'd stumbled through revealed a dark storage cupboard, the vague silhouettes of mops and brooms lining its walls.

Leah pointed towards a mop. 'There's your furry friend, George,' she said with a smile.

George grinned at her.

In the corridor, men dressed in suits hurried past them. Some gave Leah and her friends strange looks, but most ignored them, their heads buried in brown folders or deep in conversations.

'It looks like some kind of office,' Mimi mused. 'Everyone seems very . . . smart and busy.'

'Is it just me or do their suits look a bit weird?' George asked.

As the three of them watched, the corridor seemed to get even busier. Leah, Mimi and George backed up against the wall.

'We need to get out of here,' Leah murmured. Pretty soon, someone was going to demand to know what they were doing.

'Where are we going to go?' George said. 'The watch won't send us back until we've done whatever it sent us here to do. Besides, we don't even know where this office is.'

'Hey!' A loud shout came from the end of the corridor. A frazzled-looking man hurried past the children. 'Wait for me!'

A group of people further up turned towards him. 'Come on, Frank!' One of them laughed. 'We're gonna miss it!'

The man caught up with his friends and the group hurried away, talking animatedly.

'Guys! Did you hear how they spoke?' Mimi gasped. 'They were American!'

'So . . . we're in the United States?' Leah asked uncertainly.

'America is *huge*, though!' George protested. 'We could be *anywhere*!'

Leah knew that America was split up into fifty states and she'd once heard Mr Cross say that it was so big that the entirety of the United Kingdom could fit inside it forty times over. They'd have to do more detective work if they were going to work out exactly *where* the watch had deposited them, not to mention *when*. The clothes everyone was wearing looked more modern that the ones they'd seen in 1899 or 1921, but Leah couldn't be sure.

'Well,' Leah said with a sigh and a shrug. 'We're not going to figure anything out if we just stay huddled against this wall. We need to look for clues.'

'Where should we start?' George asked, trying to look like the thought of being lost somewhere in the middle of the United States wasn't anything to worry about.

'What about going . . . wherever it is they're all going?' Mimi suggested, pointing at the stream of people still flooding past them.

'Good idea,' Leah said. She stared at the men hurrying past. Their faces were filled with excitement and anticipation. It reminded Leah of how she felt when she was on her way to watch a football match.

'Is it?' said George in a high-pitched voice. 'What if someone decides we're not supposed to be here and throws us out?'

'We'll just have to be really sneaky,' Leah replied, trying to sound confident. 'If we stay close to the wall, we might be able to keep out of sight.'

George grumbled, unconvinced, but Mimi nodded. 'Let's do it!'

Mimi took a step forward, but Leah grabbed her arm. 'Wait! Does everyone have the magic items from the box?' Thanks to Rolo, Leah assumed the metal box they usually kept them all in was still on her bedroom carpet. Leah slipped the watch's chain over her neck and stashed the compass in her jumper pocket. George did the same with the key, and Mimi tucked the magnifying glass into her jeans. Leah gave a satisfied nod. 'Okay,' she said. 'Let's go.'

With Leah at the front, the three of them crept forward, keeping their heads down and trying to blend in with the crowd.

Eventually, the river of people spilled into a large, busy room. Leah, Mimi and George kept to the rear wall, whilst the adults hurried forward, pushing and jostling as though trying to get the best spot.

'Look,' George whispered, pointing towards

the front of the room. 'They look like football commentators!'

In front of the crowd were rows of desks, each with a blocky monitor perched on top of it. Sitting in front of each screen was a man wearing a bulky headset.

'I wonder what they're here for,' Mimi mused.

Suddenly the far wall flickered to life, and Leah realized that it was actually an enormous screen.

'I think we're about to find out,' she murmured as the screen flashed from blue to white and back again, until an image finally appeared: a long, white tubular shape set against a brilliant blue sky.

It was a rocket.

George gave an awed gasp. 'No way!'

A few heads turned their way and one man shushed him. George clamped his lips together, huddling closer to the wall.

Mimi's eyes glowed with excitement, but she kept her voice low as she said, 'If that's a real rocket, maybe we're in Florida, at Cape Canaveral!'

A hush fell over the room at the rocket's appearance and a tinny voice announced, '*T minus two minutes until launch.*'

'When did the first American go into space?' Leah asked Mimi in a whisper. For her birthday last year, Mimi's aunt had given her a big book on the history of space and Mimi had read it cover to cover multiple times.

Mimi frowned, thinking. '1961. His name was Alan Shepard. Why? Do you think he could be in there?' She pointed towards the rocket.

Leah bit her lip, eyes shining. 'I don't know. Anything's possible right now.'

Mimi opened her mouth to reply, but before she could say anything, the tinny voice began speaking again.

'*T minus five seconds until launch. Four . . . Three . . . Two . . .*'

It felt like the entire room was holding its breath.

'*. . . One. Launch!*'

On the screen, the rocket burst into life, tangerine-coloured flames shooting from the bottom amidst a mushroom of cloud-like smoke. Cheers erupted throughout the room as the rocket began to rise, hovering in the air as though it were being yanked up by puppeteer strings. Then it paused and began to tilt, turning onto its side.

Then it burst into flames.

Everyone froze in horror.

Less than two seconds later, with an ear-shattering bang, the entire thing exploded.

The screen went black.

Silence settled over the crowd as everyone stared at the space where, just moments before, the rocket had begun its doomed launch.

All at once, the shouting started. Men turned to each other, their voices rising louder and louder. At the desks, the workers in headsets typed frantically, their lips moving rapidly as they spoke through their microphones.

Leah, Mimi and George looked at each other, taking in what they'd just witnessed. Leah's stomach was a wriggling mess. She really hoped that no one had been inside the rocket.

She opened her mouth, but then a heavy

hand fell on her shoulder.

Mimi inhaled sharply as Leah looked up to meet the piercing stare of a moustachioed man in a security guard's uniform. His eyebrows lowered into a menacing frown as he glowered down at Leah and her friends.

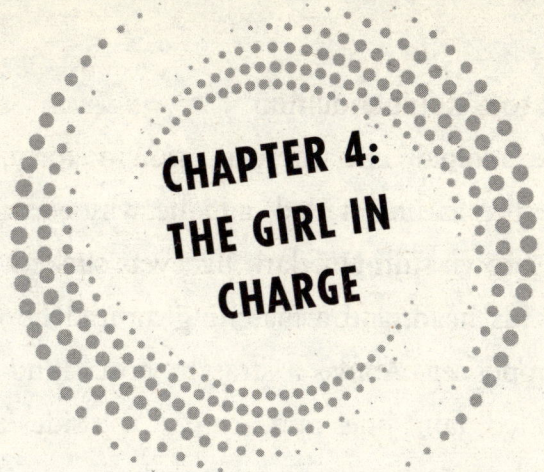

CHAPTER 4: THE GIRL IN CHARGE

'What do you kids think you're doing?' the security guard growled, his hand tightening on Leah's shoulder. 'You shouldn't be in here!'

Leah's tongue felt thick in her mouth.

'I . . . er, I mean . . . we . . .' Leah's mind had gone completely blank. It might have been easier to come up with a lie if she knew exactly when and where they were. She looked frantically at Mimi – she was normally the best in these situations – but Mimi's eyes were wide with panic as she stared up at the guard.

'What's going on here?' came a confident voice.

The security guard's head snapped up and he seemed to stand a little straighter as a white man came to a stop beside him.

He looked like he was around forty, the same age as Leah's dad, and he was wearing a crisp brown suit. His dark hair was slicked back from his head, and a matching moustache lined his upper lip. Above a straight nose, kind eyes twinkled, faint lines appearing at the sides as he cast a bemused smile down at them.

'I found these suspicious stragglers, Mr Whistler, sir,' the security guard said, his voice full of respect. 'Nothing for someone as important as the Director of the NACA to bother with, though. I can deal with them.'

'Deal with them?' Mr Whistler repeated.

The security guard puffed up his chest. 'Well, I just thought they might be—'

'Might be what?' Mr Whistler interrupted, raising one disbelieving eyebrow and tilting his head to the side. 'Soviet spies?'

The security guard blushed. 'Well, sir, I . . .'

'But, of course, you wouldn't be suggesting such a ridiculous thing. Even the Soviet Union wouldn't stoop so low as to use children to gather intel on our developing space programme.' Mr Whistler paused, running his gaze across Leah and her friends. 'And if, by chance, these children *were* Soviet spies, they aren't very good ones to have been caught out in the open like this.'

The security guard rushed to nod in agreement. 'Oh yes, sir, absolutely!'

'But that does still beg the question . . .' Mr Whistler continued as if the security guard hadn't spoken. His voice was now distinctly disapproving, and the kindness in his eyes had faded to ice. 'What on earth are you three doing here?'

'They're with me, sir!'

Leah's head whipped around as a girl materialized next to her. The girl's attention was focused on Mr Whistler, her mouth fixed into a respectful smile. She had brown skin and her dark hair was bound in two thick plaits, secured with white ribbons. She was wearing a dress the colour of buttercups, with a white collar and matching capped sleeves. On her feet, frilly ankle socks disappeared into pink pumps. There was a little pocket on the chest of her dress with what looked like a screwdriver handle sticking out, and, for a second, Leah thought she saw something move inside the pocket.

The steel in Mr Whistler's expression melted into weariness. It was the same kind of expression Leah's mum often wore when she asked Leah to do something repeatedly and Leah wasn't listening.

'Cindy,' Mr Whistler rumbled. He didn't seem surprised to see her. 'You should know better than to be running around here, especially on a day like today.'

'Oh, but I couldn't miss it, sir!' Cindy gushed, her eyes flicking to the now blank screen. Her accent was different from Mr Whistler's. His was flat and rigid, but Cindy's rolled up and down, like waves. 'And besides, my friends were real eager to see a rocket up close.'

Mr Whistler pinched the bridge of his nose. 'That may be, but you can't just bring anyone into the NACA. Am I going to have to speak to your mother about this again?'

Cindy's lips thinned and Leah thought she saw her eyes flash. 'No, sir! Please don't tell my mom! I promise it won't happen again.'

Mr Whistler narrowed his eyes and then sighed. A smile curled at the edges of his mouth. 'Well, that's good enough for me. And you'll head right back to the West Computing Area?'

'Of course, sir.' Cindy nodded. 'We'll keep out of the way. Won't we?'

For the first time, Cindy looked directly at Leah and her friends. Her dark eyes glittered in the harsh light of the control room. When Leah didn't respond immediately, they widened ever so slightly, as if urging her to play along.

'Er, yes,' Leah said finally, turning back to Mr Whistler. 'We won't cause any more trouble.'

Mr Whistler nodded. 'That's good. I've got enough to deal with here without having to worry about you four.' He looked over his shoulder at the chaos still rampaging through the room as men shouted questions and clacked loudly at their computers. The giant screen remained blank. 'Mr

Jones! Do you have any answers for me? I need an explanation for this before the President calls!' he said as he turned away.

The security guard still didn't look like he trusted them, but Cindy started marching towards the door before he could say anything.

'Come on,' she ordered.

Leah, Mimi and George looked at each other. After a second, Leah shrugged. What choice did they have? Cindy had decided to help them out and it seemed like she knew her way around. Maybe it was a smart idea to stick close to her until they could figure out why the watch had brought them here.

They followed the sound of Cindy's heels back out into the corridor. She didn't speak to them, but Leah didn't mind. Her head was whirling with everything she'd seen and heard. The image of the exploding rocket was imprinted on her brain and she kept thinking about how the flames had consumed it, the explosion happening too fast for anyone to stop it. Mr Whistler had mentioned something about the space programme, the Soviet

Union and the NACA. Leah didn't know much about any of those things, but perhaps George or Mimi did.

Cindy came to an abrupt stop outside of a door. She opened it and ushered Leah, Mimi and George inside. She came in last and then shut the door behind them.

For a second, the four of them stood in complete darkness. But then Cindy turned the light on, illuminating the room around them. Leah looked around, eager for more clues, but . . .

They were back in the cleaning cupboard.

Familiar brooms and mops lined the walls and great vats of cleaning chemicals crowded the shelves.

Leah frowned. 'What—'

Cindy rounded on her. 'I'll be asking the questions here!' she declared, her hands on her hips. 'And you three are going to answer them.'

Eyes wide, Leah looked at Mimi and George in bewilderment.

'You're going to tell me who you are and where you've come from.' Cindy sniffed. 'I've never met you and I know *everyone* at the NACA. And don't even *think* about lying to me. If you do, I'll head straight back to the control room and hand you over to Mr Whistler.'

CHAPTER 5: SPACE CAMP

Leah gulped and her mind went blank. Her mouth opened, but nothing came out.

Cindy frowned at her. 'I saw you come out of this cupboard. I want to know what you were up to in here.' She looked around the small room with a frown.

'We were looking for a broom,' Mimi suddenly blurted.

Cindy's eyes narrowed. 'Why?'

'To clean!' George replied.

'Clean what?' Cindy challenged.

'Mess, obviously,' Mimi said sarcastically.

'What mess?'

Leah looked at her friends, her mind racing. 'Uh . . . we spilled something.'

'Some juice!' George offered.

Mimi nodded eagerly. 'Yeah, we spilled some juice on the floor and we were worried someone might slip,' she said.

Leah held her breath as Cindy stared at them. She thought maybe the girl would believe them, but then Cindy shook her head, the corners of her mouth turning down.

'You're lying,' she said. She took a step back. 'The security guard was right! You *are* Soviet spies!'

'We're not!' Leah protested. 'I don't even know what that is!'

Cindy laughed. 'Only a Soviet spy would say something like that.' She crossed her arms over her chest as Leah let out a frustrated breath.

For a moment, Leah considered telling Cindy the truth. The first time the watch had taken them to the past, they'd told their friend Dot that they were from the future. She hadn't believed them to begin with, but it had made everything a lot easier. Leah stared at Cindy. She didn't know if they could trust her, but Leah felt like they were fast running out of options.

And then George started to babble.

'It's our school,' he gasped. 'They love science and space and all that stuff, so now we're here to . . . learn about it . . .' He trailed off, his eyes wide, as if even he couldn't believe the words that were tumbling from his mouth.

Leah swallowed a groan. Now they were *really* going to be in trouble. There was no way that Cindy was going to believe that three mysterious kids with English accents were here on a *school trip*. And even if she was that gullible, George was a terrible liar.

But all of the doubt suddenly disappeared from Cindy's face and her expression brightened.

'Oh! Why didn't you just say you were with the space camp kids?'

Leah looked at George and Mimi, unable to believe their luck. A space camp! That must have been why none of the office workers were that surprised to see three children roaming the halls.

Cindy didn't wait for a reply. 'I'm sorry I accused you of being Soviet spies. I didn't realize there were going to be any Brits in the school groups and my mom says you can't be too careful right now, what with the space programme and everything.'

'That's okay,' Leah said weakly.

'I suppose *your* government wants to see how well *our* government is doing in the race to get the first person into space, huh?' Cindy continued. 'And what better place to do that than in Langley, Virginia?'

Leah's heart leapt. *Virginia?*

'That's right!' Mimi was nodding along enthusiastically.

'But...' Cindy paused. 'The space camp is right over on the other side of the compound. What are you doing here in the aeronautics building?'

Now that Cindy wasn't accusing them of being spies, Mimi seemed more confident, and Leah watched as she turned on her acting skills. 'Well, it turns out that the space camp isn't as interesting as we thought it was going to be – right, guys?'

Leah and George nodded. 'We wanted to explore and we found ourselves over here.'

'Exactly,' Mimi said. 'Then we heard everyone talking about the rocket launch and we wanted to see it for ourselves!'

'Watching a rocket take off is way cooler than just learning about it,' Cindy agreed. She bit her lip. 'It's just a shame that it didn't actually manage to, you know, *take off*.'

'What happened to it?' George asked.

Cindy shrugged. 'Who knows? The scientists and mathematicians will be trying to figure that out now.' She sighed wistfully. 'Imagine. 1957. The year the United States of America launched the first rocket into the Earth's orbit . . .'

Leah's eyes snapped to her friends. That was it! The watch had transported them to 1957!

'Anyway,' Cindy said, shrugging her shoulders as though she were shaking off her disappointment. 'We should probably get you three back to the camp before your teacher notices you're gone.'

Leah looked at her friends and they all shook their heads. 'It's, uh, really busy over there,' she said, thinking quickly. 'There are too many children there for her to notice anything.'

'Oh!' Cindy said brightly. 'Does that mean you've got some time to explore? I know that, after today, the camp is only running for another two days. I don't want you to miss it.'

'We don't mind!' Mimi replied quickly.

Cindy beamed. 'Swell! There aren't usually many kids around here. It would be nice to have some company. And I can give you the inside scoop on what *really* goes on at the National Advisory Committee for Aeronautics.' She puffed her chest up importantly.

'The National Advisory thingy for what?' Mimi said, raising an eyebrow.

'You know,' Cindy laughed. 'The NACA!'

'Oh, right,' Leah said, wrinkling her nose. 'Of course.'

'Come on!' Cindy said, striding to the cupboard door. 'I'll be your guide for the afternoon. By the end of the day, you'll know everything there is to know about the space programme!'

CHAPTER 6: THE WEST COMPUTING GROUP

Leah, Mimi and George followed Cindy back out into the corridor. It was much calmer now that the rocket launch was over.

As they walked, Mimi caught up with Leah, nudging her shoulder. 'I've heard of the NACA,' she whispered. 'It was in the book my aunt gave me. Anyway, the NACA becomes NASA.'

'As in the NASA that launches rockets into space in our time?' Leah asked.

Mimi nodded. 'That's right.'

'What are you two muttering about?' Cindy called over her shoulder. 'Come on!'

She led them around a corner and out into a large glass-fronted lobby. A security guard wearing a camel-coloured uniform and matching hat was sitting behind a desk close to the main entrance and Cindy gave him a friendly wave as they passed.

They emerged onto a set of steps by a large car park. The cars were nothing like those Leah was used to seeing at home. They were squat and rectangular and some of them even had strange sweeping fins at the back, on either side of the boot.

'Afternoon, Apollo!' Cindy said in a cheerful voice as she skipped down the concrete steps. She tilted her head like she was tipping an imaginary hat.

When Leah followed her, it became clear that she wasn't speaking to a person, but to a dog. It was a Labrador retriever, its coat a shiny gold. Its tail *thwump*ed happily at the sight of Cindy, but when it noticed Leah and her friends, its lips curled back from gleaming canines and it let out an angry bark.

'Huh,' Mimi said, tilting her head to the side. 'Dogs usually love me.'

'Oh, don't take it personally!' Cindy assured her as they left Apollo behind. 'He's a total sweetheart, but he doesn't take kindly to strangers. Once he gets to know you, he's a big old softie.'

'Who does he belong to?' Leah asked.

'Bert, the security guard on the desk. Apollo's been coming to work with him since he was a puppy,' Cindy replied.

Leaving Apollo behind, the four of them traipsed around the edge of the car park. Leah paused as she felt a jolt of pain in her knee, but after a few careful stretches, the pain faded and she followed the others into a warren of concrete buildings. As they passed, Cindy named them all, reeling off a list of long and complicated titles that Leah forgot as soon as she heard them. She peeped through the windows and could see more men in suits busy at their desks or standing in front of enormous blackboards.

'Is everyone who works here trying to get a rocket into space?' George asked.

Cindy nodded. 'Of course! What else would they be doing?'

Without waiting for an answer, Cindy led them down a narrow pathway between two brown, boxy offices. A chill wind whipped along the pavement and Leah shivered, wrapping her arms around herself. She wished she were wearing jeans like George and Mimi, but her mum had insisted on shorts whilst her knee was healing because they were less restrictive. Leah was grateful for her grey hoody, though. She pulled the cuffs down over her hands and hugged them to her chest.

It seemed that Cindy had noticed their clothes, too. 'Gee, I wish my mom would let me wear jeans or shorts like you guys, but she says that it's unladylike.' Cindy's eyes widened. 'I mean . . . not that you look unladylike or anything!'

Leah laughed. 'It's okay,' she said. She was relieved that the watch had brought them back to a time where they didn't have to change into new clothes. The dress in 1921 had been so itchy!

'Are we nearly there?' Mimi said finally, after they'd been following Cindy for a while. 'We've been walking for ages. This place can't be that big!' They were still surrounded by buildings. It was as though the compound were growing around them the further they went.

'Actually, it *is* that big,' Cindy said, coming to a stop. 'There's about a mile between the Aeronautics building and the West Computing Area.'

'Whoa,' George said. 'That's further than it is from my house to yours, Leah.'

'Well, how much longer is it going to take?' Mimi said impatiently. Leah was also keen to stop walking. Her knee had begun to ache again.

Cindy grinned, and then gestured in front of them. 'We're here!'

Leah looked at the blocky building. Its walls were a dark grey and a small path cut through a perfectly manicured lawn, leading up to a set of double doors. Above them was a plaque with the words 'West Computing Area' printed on it.

George squinted and read the sign aloud. Then he said, 'Does that mean there's an East Computing Area, too?'

'Yeah,' Cindy answered, and then she shrugged. 'But that's only for white women. Black folks, like my mom, have to work over here.'

'You're not allowed to sit together? Because of the colour of your skin?' Mimi asked, her eyebrows raised in disbelief. 'That's not fair!'

Cindy gave a sad smile. 'That's just the way it is here. The mathematicians are split up.'

'Is that what your mum does?' Leah asked. 'Maths?'

'She sure does.' Cindy beamed. 'In fact, she's the best mathematician in this whole place! If you come with me, you can meet her.'

Suddenly, George let out a yelp and took a step backwards. He raised a single finger towards the pocket on Cindy's dress. 'There's a worm in there!' he cried. 'I just saw it!'

Leah looked. At first, she couldn't see anything apart from the screwdriver handle, but then something worm-like *did* flick out of the top of Cindy's pocket.

Cindy didn't seem worried, though. In fact, she laughed.

'It's not a worm!' She giggled. She moved the screwdriver out of the way and reached into her pocket, scooping something out. 'It's Marty!'

Curled in the centre of her palm was a little mouse. His fur was the colour of ash and two tiny raisin-like eyes blinked up at Leah. What George had mistaken for a worm was actually Marty's tail. It curved around his little body in an S shape.

'He's so cute!' Mimi squealed, clapping her hands together.

His full name is Martian,' Cindy told them, stroking a finger down Marty's back.

The mouse rubbed his nose between his paws, whiskers twitching. 'But Mom and I call him Marty for short.'

'Why do you have a *mouse* for a pet?' George said, wrinkling his nose as he kept his distance.

Cindy shrugged. 'A dog is too big and Mom's not a cat person. Besides, I *like* mice.'

A cold wind rustled the grass and Marty shivered. He turned and scampered up Cindy's arm, travelling across her shoulder and then dropping down into her pocket. His head poked up over the edge, beady eyes staring out.

'Come on, then,' Cindy said, clapping her hands together. 'I want you guys to meet my mom.'

They headed into the building. Inside, it was smaller than Leah had expected and, unlike the Aeronautics building, there wasn't a grand lobby or a reception desk. Instead, they found themselves in a dimly lit corridor with no windows. Immediately, Cindy set off down the hallway.

Soon, the sound of raised voices echoed along the corridor.

'You've made a mistake and now you need to accept responsibility!'

'Excuse me? Are you accusing me of—'

'Oh no,' muttered Cindy.

'What's wrong?' Leah asked. 'Who is that?'

Cindy sighed. 'No one good.' She turned a corner, bringing them to an open doorway.

Inside was a large room filled with desks. Each desk held a machine that looked a bit like a typewriter, but instead of paper coming out of the top, it had what looked like a chunky ruler balancing on the box. Dozens of Black women sat at the desks, their fingertips poised over the keys. But none of them were typing. Instead, they were staring at two figures in the centre of the room.

One was a woman that Leah knew must be Cindy's mother. The resemblance between the two was obvious, from the gently sloping nose to the deep pools of her dark eyes. Her thick hair was curled and elegantly pinned up atop her head with a tortoiseshell clip and she wore a neatly pressed blouse tucked into a green checked skirt.

Her lips were painted a bright fuchsia.

Opposite her was a tall, thin man. His hair was black and slicked back with so much grease it gleamed. Thick-rimmed glasses perched on the end of his narrow nose. Like most of the men Leah had seen at the NACA, he was white and wearing a crisp black suit. He clutched a wad of papers in his hand.

The two of them faced off against each other like opponents in a boxing ring.

'Who's that man?' Leah whispered, leaning close to Cindy's ear.

'That's Mr Jones,' Cindy replied darkly, her eyes flinty beneath her lowered brow. 'He's Mr Whistler's right-hand man. The lead engineer on the whole project.'

'My calculations were not wrong, Mr Jones,' Cindy's mum was saying, her eyes flashing.

'There are chunks of blown-up rocket littering the ground in Florida which disagree, Mrs Grant,' Mr Jones growled, eyebrows raised. 'You made an error!'

'Well, sir, I can only work with the numbers your physicists and engineers have given me. If

there's an error to be found, I suggest you start there.' Mrs Grant tilted her chin up. 'Although perhaps you've lost all of your *best* men. I've heard they're all leaving!'

Her words sent a shiver of fury through Mr Jones. 'How dare you? The men in my department have educational backgrounds that put yours to shame—'

'Oh yes,' Mrs Grant interrupted, rolling her eyes. 'Only because none of those colleges will admit women into their classes, let alone Black people!'

There was a murmur throughout the room as the women sitting at the desks nodded their agreement.

Mr Jones waved his hand dismissively. 'And for good reason! I should have listened to my gut. A woman's calculations cannot be trusted, especially a Black woman's. I never would have involved you, if not for Mr Whistler's insistence. And now look where it's got us. I bet the Soviets are laughing themselves sick!'

'Oh, come on now. Arguing like this isn't going to solve anything!' A woman that Leah hadn't noticed before stepped out from Mr Jones's shadow. She was taller than Cindy's mum and her skin was as pale as the papers she was holding in her hands. Her mousy brown hair was scraped back into a bun and she wore a cream cardigan over a flowery dress. She looked pleadingly between the two arguing figures. 'This has all just been a misunderstanding.'

'When it comes to math, there are no misunderstandings, Miss Sinclair,' Mr Jones sniped. 'Something is either right, or it is wrong.'

Miss Sinclair shook her head. 'Please don't make me report this to Mr Whistler. As his personal assistant, I am duty-bound to tell him about any issues, and I know he'd be so disappointed to hear that you'd been at odds.'

As she spoke, Miss Sinclair's arms flapped at her sides. With her last sentence, they'd risen higher, and with one expressive flick of her wrists, a tall stack of papers arranged on the edge of the nearest desk went flying.

Flustered, Miss Sinclair bent to retrieve them, but Cindy's mum and Mr Jones didn't pay her any attention. They were too focused on each other. Cindy's mum's expression was defiant and it only seemed to be making Mr Jones angrier.

He pointed a finger towards her. 'You will fix this. I want a solution by the end of the day!'

'Don't be ridiculous!' Cindy's mum scoffed, her hands on her hips. 'We can't rush this. It'll be a disaster if we do. People could get hurt!'

'I. Don't. Care!' Mr Jones snarled, punctuating each word with a thrust of his finger. 'I want a solution, Mrs Grant, or who knows what will happen to you next.'

He spun on his heel and marched towards the door, where Leah and her friends were still loitering. 'Get out of my way!' he snarled. They'd barely had a chance to move before he bouldered past them and out into the corridor.

'What a blockhead,' Cindy muttered, glaring at his back. 'Come on.'

She led Leah and her friends into the room and over to where her mum was standing, her hand braced against a desk.

'Don't worry about that,' she was saying to Miss Sinclair, who was still scrabbling about on the floor. The personal assistant surged to her feet, patting the papers back into a neat pile and replacing them on the desk.

'I did try to stop him coming over here,' she said with a shake of her head. Now that she was closer, Leah could see that the collar of her cream cardigan was covered in little badges, all in the shape of the American flag. 'Mr Whistler will be frightfully angry when I tell him what's happened.'

'Oh no, don't you bother Mr Whistler with this,' Cindy's mum replied. 'He has bigger things on his plate.'

Miss Sinclair seemed like she wanted to say more, but then she caught sight of the children. 'Looks like you've got company,' she said. 'I'll see you later. Are we still on for dinner this Friday?'

Cindy's mum smiled. 'Yes, ma'am. Same as every week.'

Miss Sinclair patted her shoulder and then waved at the children as she passed them on her way out.

'Mom!' Cindy rushed forward and grabbed her hand. 'Are you okay?'

'Oh, honey,' her mum sighed. 'Did you see all that? I'm so sorry!'

'Was Mr Jones telling the truth? Was your math the reason the rocket blew up?' Cindy looked up at her mother and Leah saw her face flood with relief when Mrs Grant shook her head firmly.

'Absolutely not. But let's not talk about that right now.' Her eyes flickered to Leah, Mimi and George. 'Who are your friends?'

Cindy brightened. 'This is Leah, Mimi and George; they're from the space camp. I'm giving them a tour!'

'Ah! Nice to meet you all, I'm Nancy, Cindy's mom, although you probably already know that!' Nancy cried, her eyes twinkling. 'So you're interested in space? You've come to the right place!'

'What's your job here?' Leah asked politely, looking around the room. There was a big blackboard at one end covered in chalk calculations, and the shelves next to it were full of books about maths. 'Cindy said you're a mathematician but—'

'The plaque outside says this is the West Computing Area – why don't you have any computers on your desks?' George interrupted.

Nancy tipped her head back and laughed. 'Those are some pretty big questions! I think I can answer them, though.' She tapped her finger against her lips as she looked at the clock on the wall. 'I've had enough of this place for the day. You kids wanna grab a burger? I'm starving!'

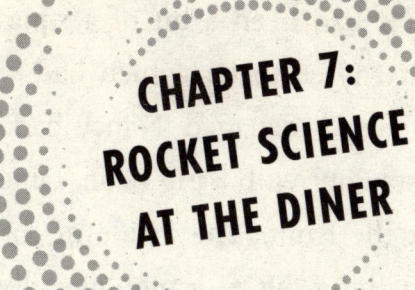

CHAPTER 7: ROCKET SCIENCE AT THE DINER

'So, you're part of the space camp, huh?' Nancy said. She took a massive bite of her burger. Mustard dripped out of the bottom and splattered onto her plate.

'Er, yeah,' Leah said, scooping two fries through a dollop of ketchup.

'Well, that's wonderful.' Nancy beamed. 'I think it's really neat that the government is trying to get kids interested in science, even kids from overseas. It's the future of this nation and the whole world – isn't that right, Cindy?'

'It sure is.' Cindy nodded as she fed Marty a fry.

After they'd left the West Computing Area, the four children had piled into the back of

Nancy's car. It had been a bit of a squash and there weren't any seatbelts, which had worried George, but they'd managed. Nancy had driven them to a restaurant with a big neon 'Diner' sign blinking out the front. The inside of the diner was like something out of a film. The floor was tiled in a black-and-white chequered pattern and a red counter curved through the middle. Scarlet booths lined the walls, their vinyl seats shining. They'd all slid into one and ordered burgers and milkshakes.

'Have you been at the NACA long?' Mimi asked. There hadn't been a vegetarian option so her burger sat abandoned to one side of her plate.

'About eight years,' Nancy replied.

'Wow, that's ages!' said George. 'You must know loads about space!'

'I know the basics.' Nancy chuckled. 'But mostly, I just work with the numbers the engineers give me.'

'Mom, come on!' Cindy rolled her eyes. 'Without you and everyone in the West Computing Area,

there wouldn't *be* any rocket launches.'

'What does the West Computing Area do?' Leah asked.

'And why aren't there any computers there?' George piped up.

'There are computers,' Nancy said with a mysterious smile. She took a slurp of her milkshake and then pointed at her chest. 'I'm a computer.'

George frowned in confusion. 'Er, what?'

Nancy laughed. 'What other kinds of computers are there?'

'You know, like, a machine with screens and keyboards?' George's voice was full of bewilderment.

'Oh, *them*?' Nancy laughed. 'No, I'm not talking about those strange boxes. What use are they when it comes to math?'

'Mom!' Cindy interrupted. 'I like those computers.'

Nancy rolled her eyes. 'I know you do, but they're just not smart enough to do the calculations as fast as we can. And besides, they're too expensive to use across the whole of the NACA. You'll only really find them in the control room. Us women in the West Computing Area – we're what they call *human* computers. We run all of the mathematical calculations for the space programme.'

'But . . . but . . .' George sputtered. 'That can't be right! I *saw* all those typewriter things on your desks.'

Nancy popped some fries in her mouth and

shook her head whilst she chewed and swallowed. 'Those aren't keyboards *or* typewriters. They're calculators! They help us when we're working on complex math, but we do most of it mentally.'

Leah looked at George and Mimi, her eyes wide as she tried to understand what Nancy was saying. Back home, calculators were small enough to fit in her pocket, although she usually used the one on her phone.

'So . . .' Mimi said slowly. 'You do all of those sums in your head?' Her voice was full of awe.

'Not all of them, but most of them.' Nancy smiled.

'But isn't that really hard?' Leah blurted. She liked maths, but the thought of doing every calculation mentally was daunting.

'Sometimes.' Nancy shrugged. 'But really, the math you need to know for rocket science isn't that difficult. Cindy, why don't you explain it to them?'

Cindy leaned forward eagerly. 'It's a basic formula, really. Force equals mass times acceleration.'

Nancy nodded. 'Newton's second law of motion.'

George gaped at them. 'I feel like you've started talking in a different language.' Cindy and Nancy laughed.

'Sorry,' Cindy said with an apologetic shrug. 'I spend so much time at the NACA with Mom and the other computers that I forget not everyone speaks math. But I promise it really is more simple than it seems. Let me start at the beginning. Have you heard of Newton's laws of motion?'

Leah, Mimi and George shook their heads.

'Okay, well, the laws of motion are three rules that we can apply to anything if we want it to move,' Cindy explained.

'Like forces?' Leah asked. They'd learned all about forces in science at school.

'Exactly!' Cindy beamed. 'Push, pull, that kind of thing. The first law says that an object will not change its motion unless a force is applied to it. The second law is all about how fast an object is going and the amount of force needed to make it accelerate, and the third law is about action and reaction. You know, when a force is applied to an object, the opposite force is created as a reaction. Are you following?'

George frowned. 'Er, kind of?'

'Ow. My brain hurts.' Mimi rubbed her forehead.

Leah grinned. 'Mimi's right. I don't think it's as easy as you make it seem!'

Cindy laughed. 'Sorry. I'm a bit of nerd when it comes to math and science. My mom's taught me well! Basically, all you need to know is that the laws of motion have to be followed if a rocket is going to be launched successfully into space.'

'So, when Mr Jones was shouting at you, it was because something had gone *wrong* with the laws of motion?' George asked.

Nancy frowned and shook her head. 'He *thought* something had gone wrong. But my math was solid. I used the numbers he gave me and I *know* all my calculations were correct.'

'Is there a chance one of the other computers made a mistake?' Mimi asked, but Nancy shook her head.

'I do all my calculations myself, and I write them up, too. I don't trust anyone else.' She sighed. 'Mr Jones knows that, but he just doesn't want to take responsibility and accept that there might be a deeper problem.'

'But . . . why?' Leah asked, bewildered.

'Because deeper problems take more time to solve,' Nancy explained. 'You see, rockets aren't built to be reused. They have one job – to create enough thrust to enter the Earth's orbit. When that job is done, the rocket breaks up so that the debris doesn't cause any problems as it falls back to Earth.'

'But what about if a person is inside?' Mimi interrupted.

Nancy smiled. 'None of the rockets hold people right now. We haven't figured out a way to keep humans safe inside. Our rockets are *meant* to explode, just not immediately after launch. If Mr Jones accepts today's failure isn't because of the math, he and his team will have to work harder to find out what the problem is. That takes time, though, and President Eisenhower is putting a lot of pressure on the department. He wants results and he wants them now.' Nancy shook her head.

Leah opened her mouth to ask why, but at that moment, a waitress appeared at their table. Her blonde hair was elegantly curled and tucked up underneath a white headband, and her red apron and white dress matched the booths they were sat in. She beamed down at them, her teeth shining.

'Can I get you folks anything else to eat? Some dessert maybe?'

Cindy clapped her hands together in excitement. 'Oh, Mom, can I get some cherry pie?' She turned to Leah, George and Mimi, her eyes wide. 'You've got to try it. It's the best pie I've *ever* tasted.'

Nancy ordered four pies and a black coffee for herself.

'Mr Jones is only upset because he doesn't want us to lose the race, Mom,' Cindy said, once the waitress had disappeared.

'What race?' Leah asked.

Cindy looked at her strangely. 'The Space Race, of course! We're in a competition with the

Soviet Union to see who can get a person into space first. And we're going to win, too!' She clenched her hand into a determined fist.

'The Soviet Union?' Leah asked cautiously. Since they'd arrived in the past, she'd heard the word 'Soviet' more times than she could count, and she still wasn't any closer to understanding what it meant.

Cindy looked at her like she'd spouted a second head. 'You've never heard of the Soviet Union?'

Leah felt her cheeks flame. 'Well, I mean, we've *heard* of it. We're just not quite sure what it means.'

'The Soviet Union is a collection of countries in Europe that have joined together. The largest one is Russia and smaller countries like Ukraine and Belarus are part of it, too,' Nancy explained kindly. 'And they're determined to win the Space Race. President Eisenhower, however, isn't willing to let that happen. The whole country is in some kind of space frenzy.'

Cindy looked at her mum. 'You want us to win too, don't you, Mom?'

Nancy started to answer but paused as the waitress appeared with their pies and Nancy's coffee. Once she'd left, Nancy took a gulp of her drink and then set the cup down carefully. 'Of course I do, but this race means that the NACA are working faster than ever and Mr Whistler is under tremendous pressure.' She sighed and rubbed the side of her head. 'I just don't want our impatience to get the better of us. We shouldn't be cutting corners. Winning isn't all that matters.'

'What's more important than winning?' Leah asked with a frown. She took a bite of her pie. The sweet, tangy taste of cherry filled her mouth. It was absolutely delicious!

Nancy was quiet and she shook her head, sighing. 'I'm afraid that if we're not careful and only focus on winning . . . well, I'm worried that people are going to get hurt.'

CHAPTER 8: AMERICAN FOOTBALL

After they'd all finished their food and Nancy had paid the bill, they all traipsed back to the car.

'Where are you kids staying?' she asked Leah, Mimi and George as she rummaged in her handbag for her car keys. 'At the dorms on the compound?'

'Um...' Leah glanced at her friends, biting her lip. They hadn't even thought about where they were going to stay for the night. 'I—'

'Hey, you guys should come and stay at our house! We could have a sleepover!' Cindy beamed. Marty had climbed out of her pocket to perch on her shoulder and the little mouse twitched his ears as if in agreement.

'Cindy!' Nancy reprimanded her. 'I'm sure

their teacher wouldn't be very happy about that.'

'Actually,' Mimi said quickly, 'I don't think she'd mind at all. They don't even take a register before bed.'

Nancy gave them a hard look. 'We should still let them know.' She looked around and spotted a payphone by the door to the diner. 'I'll give them a call.'

She started to stride forward, but Leah quickly stepped in her way. There was no way they could let Nancy get to that phone.

Nancy raised her eyebrow.

'Um, don't worry!' Leah said. 'We'll call them for you. I've got the number in my pocket.'

Nancy was silent, but then she nodded. 'Okay, fine. Meet us in the car when you're done. Do you have the right change?'

Leah nodded and patted the side of her shorts. 'Yes, we'll be quick!'

Leaving Nancy and Cindy by the car, Leah, Mimi and George hurried towards the payphone. It didn't look anything like the phones at home. There was a circular dial on the front and the phone hung from a hook on the side.

'What are we going to do now?' George hissed. 'There's no one to call!'

Mimi flicked her braids over her shoulder and tilted her chin up. 'Oh, George. That doesn't matter when you've got an actress for a best friend.'

They reached the phone and Mimi took it off the hook. Then she pretended to turn the dial

on the front of the phone. Leah looked over her shoulder to see that Nancy was standing against the bonnet of the car, watching them.

'Oh hi, miss!' Mimi said loudly. 'Yes, we're sorry we weren't there for dinner. That's right, we met the director of the NACA himself and now we're with one of the human computers. She'd like us to stay over. Would that be okay?'

Leah gripped her hands together tightly as she listened to Mimi. As usual, her performance was very convincing, but Leah still wasn't sure it would work. If it were Leah's mum, there was no way she'd be happy unless she'd talked to the teacher herself. Although, Leah supposed, maybe things were different in 1957.

Mimi slammed the receiver back down and turned to them with a broad smile. She waved over at Nancy and called, 'She said it's okay!'

Nancy nodded and she opened the car door. They hurried back over to find Cindy already scrunched up against the far window. As they slid inside to join her, Nancy muttered, 'I'll speak to her tomorrow. After all, the camp's only on for two more days and I don't want you kids to miss out.'

Leah's stomach plummeted. What were they going to do when Nancy went over to the space camp and realized that they'd made the whole thing up?

Cindy's house was on a quiet street about twenty minutes' drive from the diner. Nancy parked the car and they all piled onto the path. The house was narrow, with a white porch. A rocking chair sat next to the front door, looking out over the small front garden. The sun had almost disappeared below the horizon, casting the house in dusky shadows.

Nancy started to lead them inside, but Cindy paused at the porch steps. 'Do you mind if we stay out here for a while, Mom?'

Nancy hesitated and glanced at her watch. Finally, she nodded. 'Not too late, though,' she warned, and slipped inside.

Cindy headed towards the lawn, collapsing on the grass. Leah, Mimi and George sank down beside her.

'What a day,' Cindy breathed. 'We were *thiiis* close to launching that rocket.' She held her thumb and her forefinger up, a centimetre apart.

'I'm sure the next rocket launch will be much better,' George said, trying to be reassuring.

'Maybe.' Cindy sighed. She turned on her side, the white ribbons in her plaits trailing against the grass. 'Anyway, what do you guys do in your spare time when you aren't at space camp?'

'Well,' Mimi said. 'Leah and I like to play football.'

Cindy raised her eyebrow. 'Football? Really? Do they let girls play that where you're from?'

'Of course,' Leah said, smiling. 'Why? Do girls not play football here?'

Cindy shook her head. 'Definitely not!'

Mimi suddenly jumped to her feet, her arms swinging at her sides. 'Well, why don't we break the rules a little bit? Do you have a football?'

Cindy frowned thoughtfully. 'I think my dad has one.'

'Do you think we could borrow it?' Leah said eagerly, pushing herself to her feet. The thought of even holding a football in her hands filled her with excitement.

'Of course! I'm sure he won't mind us using it without him,' Cindy said with a grin. She sprang up and sprinted up the stairs and into the house.

'You should be careful,' George said to Leah, looking pointedly at her knee. 'You don't want to hurt yourself even more.'

'I'll be fine!' Leah said, waving her hand dismissively. 'But quick, before Cindy gets back, have either of you seen any clues that might explain why the watch brought us here?'

'You mean other than the gigantic exploding rocket?' Mimi said, raising her eyebrow.

'I don't think it can be to do with that,' Leah scoffed. 'We don't know enough about rockets to stop that happening again.'

'Well, other than that . . .' Mimi trailed off, shrugging. 'I've got nothing.'

'Me neither,' George said.

Leah bit her lip. How were they supposed to get home if they had no idea what it was they were supposed to do in 1957? Sometimes she wished the watch could talk. Then she could just *ask* it what it wanted her to do.

'We'll just have to keep an eye out,' she said finally with a sigh. 'But we'd better work it out soon. The space camp ends in two days and then we'll have no reason to be here.'

'That's if Nancy doesn't figure out we're not telling the truth first,' George added. 'If she contacts anyone at the camp . . .'

'Then we're in big trouble,' Mimi finished solemnly.

'I've got it!' Cindy suddenly shouted from the front step. She was holding something in her hand. It was brown and vaguely oval, with slightly pointed ends.

Leah frowned. 'Where's the football?'

'What do you mean? It's here!' Cindy giggled. She held the strange brown thing out again.

'Oh!' George cried in realization. 'That's an *American* football!'

Cindy laughed as she skipped down the steps towards them. 'Of course it is! We *are* in America after all.'

'Uh, we don't know how to play American football,' Leah said, rubbing the back of her head uncertainly. 'We were talking about what you call soccer.'

Cindy pulled a face. 'Well, I don't know how to play that. And I don't have a soccer ball anyway.' She laughed as Leah, Mimi and George looked at each other doubtfully. 'It's not that hard,' she assured them. 'Come on, I'll teach you.'

For the next hour, Cindy did her best to explain American football. She positioned Leah, Mimi and George around the lawn, showing them where to move and how to throw the ball. Leah didn't fully understand all the rules, but it was still good fun. By the time George finally managed to dodge around Cindy's attempts at defence and slam the ball on either side of the stick they were using as a goal marker, their stomachs were sore from laughing.

That wasn't the only thing that was sore, though.

As George finished his victory lap, Leah's knee gave a sharp twinge and she hissed. She'd

done her best not to run too energetically, but it seemed that even the limited amount of exercise she'd done had been too much.

'Are you okay, L?' Mimi said.

Leah gave a strained smile.

'Yeah, I think I just need to rest.' She sighed. 'I can't wait until I can just play properly again. It's so annoying having to be careful all the time.'

'We know,' George said. 'But you have to be

patient. If you do too much too soon, it could make your knee worse. Then you won't be able to play *at all*.'

'I know, I know. It's just . . . frustrating.' She rubbed at her bandage.

George slung his arm around Leah's shoulder and grinned at her. 'Just think how good it'll feel, though, the first time you step back on the pitch.'

Leah smiled. In her mind, she saw the school field, the crisp white lines, the opposing team. And in the middle, the football waiting for her.

Nancy had arranged blankets and sleeping bags on the floor of Cindy's bedroom. Leah, Mimi and George would sleep there, whilst Cindy took her bed. The curtains were drawn, but even in the dim lighting, Leah could still see that the walls were covered in posters of rockets and that books about space lined the shelves. There was a desk covered in what looked like mounds of plastic, wires and tools.

'What's that?' George said, leaning over the mess of electronics. He reached his hand forward, but Cindy grabbed his fingers.

'Don't touch it!' she cried. 'It's my computer!'

'I thought your mum said that computers are useless,' Leah said.

'Well, they're not!' Cindy replied defensively. 'She's just old-fashioned. I think computers are *fascinating*. And I have a feeling everyone is going to be using them in the future. My dad found this one in a dumpster.' She bit her lip. 'I'm pretty sure it's broken, but I'm taking it apart so I can fix it!'

Nancy appeared in the doorway. 'I've got to head back to the office for a little while,' she told them. 'They've just called me in. But Gramma is in the lounge, so if you need anything, you can call her, okay?'

'Okay, Mom,' Cindy said with a yawn. 'Don't work too hard.'

Nancy smiled softly and shut the door, leaving the four of them to bury themselves beneath the covers. Cindy deposited Marty into his cage before she got into bed.

'Your mum works a lot,' Leah said once they

were all settled. 'She must really love her job.'

'She does,' Cindy replied. 'But she doesn't normally work *this* much. Things have been so busy since the Space Race started.'

'Do you want to be a human computer too?' Mimi asked, turning onto her side.

Cindy shook her head. 'Nope, I'm going to be an engineer. The first *Black female* engineer at the NACA!'

'You mean . . . out of all the engineers working at the compound, none of them are women?'

'Well, there was a white woman called Kitty O'Brien Joyner, but other than that, they're all men. Women – especially Black women – aren't allowed to go to the schools that give the qualifications you need to become an engineer,' Cindy replied.

'That's so unfair!' Leah cried.

'I know.' Cindy sighed. 'But it's okay because I'm going to change it all. I'm going to be right there on the front line of space exploration. The first girl to help build a rocket.'

'That would be so cool,' Leah whispered.

Cindy began to snore softly and Leah turned on her side so that she was facing Mimi and George.

'Do you think that's why we're here?' she whispered. 'To help Cindy become an engineer?'

'Hmm,' Mimi said thoughtfully. 'I'm not sure. Cindy isn't old enough yet, so we'd be stuck here forever.'

'I know,' Leah said. 'But I can't see what else we're supposed to do.'

'It *is* a bit of a mystery,' George said, taking his glasses off.

'I'm sure we'll find out soon,' Mimi said confidently. 'We just need to trust that the watch has brought us here for a reason.'

As Leah rolled over, sleep making her arms and legs heavy, she hoped that Mimi was right and that they worked it out before it was too late.

CHAPTER 9: GONE GIRL

In the morning, when Leah and her friends woke up and tumbled out of bed, Nancy was nowhere to be found.

Cindy didn't seem concerned. 'Well, she did say there was a lot of work to get done at the office,' she said as the four of them wandered into the kitchen. 'Maybe she went in early. Did you see her, Gramma?'

She addressed this question to an older woman who was bustling around the small kitchen, juggling plates and cups. Her curly, grey-streaked hair had been pulled back into a bun and her eyes smiled at them from behind thin wire spectacles.

'Not me,' Gramma said, placing a large dish of

scrambled eggs on the table. 'She was gone when I got up, too.'

Cindy let out a low, impressed whistle as she heaped eggs onto her plate. Marty was perched on her shoulder, and Cindy fed him a small crumb of toast. 'Wow, she must have got up *really* early. It takes a lot to beat Gramma out of bed.'

'But . . . if your mum's gone, how are we going to get to the compound?' Leah asked.

'We'll take the bus,' Cindy said happily. 'It's not that far.'

After that, they ate in a contented silence. Gramma had made them a feast, with eggs, and bacon, and piles of hot, buttery toast. There was also a big bowl full of fried, cubed potatoes that Cindy called 'home fries'. They were covered in salt and rosemary, and Leah thought they were so delicious she took a second helping.

When their plates were empty, Gramma handed Cindy four neatly wrapped sandwiches, which Cindy stashed in her bag. Then Leah, Mimi and George followed her out of the house towards the bus stop, shouting goodbye to Gramma as they left.

The bus stop was only a short walk from the house. Unlike at home, there was no shelter, just a tall pole with a sign on it detailing the bus times. Luckily, there was a yellow bus trundling down the road just as they arrived. It came to a stop in front of them, its door opening with a *whoosh*. Cindy had borrowed some change from Gramma and she placed the coins in a little dish with a *clink*. In return, the driver gave her four tickets.

The bus wasn't busy and they found four seats together near the front. The plastic coating crinkled beneath Leah's legs as she sat. Outside the window, the buildings of Langley flashed by in a brown-grey blur.

'I love sitting at the front of the bus. You know, not that long ago, we wouldn't have been able to sit here,' Cindy told them, as the bus pulled up at the next stop to let new passengers on.

'What, on the bus?' George asked, confused.

'We'd have been allowed on the bus, but we'd have had to sit back there,' Cindy replied, waving her hand over her shoulder. 'Until a few years ago, the front of the bus was only for white folks.'

'What?' Leah said. 'That's so unfair!'

Cindy nodded. 'Those were the rules. But then a Black lady down in Montgomery, Alabama, sat at the front after a long day at work and refused to move. She wasn't the first person to decide she'd had enough of the laws, but this time, lots of other people and organizations decided they'd had enough, too. They supported her when the police arrested her.'

'Rosa Parks!' Mimi whispered.

'That's right,' Cindy said, surprised. 'I didn't realize you'd heard about her over in England.'

George nodded. 'Uh, yeah, we know all about her.'

'Then you'll know that after she refused to move, most of the Black people in Montgomery protested. They refused to ride the buses at all until they could sit wherever they like,' Cindy said.

'It's ridiculous to stop someone doing something just because of the colour of their skin,' Mimi said, and Leah nodded in agreement.

Her body fizzed with anger.

Cindy gave her a sad smile. '*We* know that, but for lots of people living here, the colour of your skin is the only thing they see. But we're going to change that. My mom says we all have to do our bit to change the world for the better.'

'I think she's right,' Leah said quietly. 'And if we want anything to change, we've got to work hard to make it happen.'

'Hey,' George said suddenly, sitting up straighter and squinting out of the window at a familiar cluster of buildings, visible beyond a chain fence. 'Is that the compound?'

'Oh!' Cindy gasped. 'We almost missed it!' She pressed the bell to let the driver know they wanted to get off and jumped up. 'Come on!'

They piled onto the pavement and the bus drove away. Leah, George and Mimi walked behind Cindy as she led them along the perimeter of the fence until they reached a guard hut with a barrier that opened to allow cars to pass through. Leah expected the security guard to stop them, but when he saw Cindy, he just waved them through with a lazy flick of his hand.

'We should probably head over to the space camp,' Cindy said. 'We can let your teachers know you're here first, and then we can go and find my mom.'

Leah's stomach knotted with panic. There was no way they could let Cindy get anywhere near that camp. 'Oh, we don't need to go yet,' she said, trying to sound confident. 'They'll probably still be at breakfast. Why don't we go and find your mum first?'

Cindy frowned. 'Are you sure?'

'Yes, we want to thank her for letting us stay!' Mimi replied eagerly.

Cindy thought about this for a moment, but finally she shrugged.

Leah looked at George and Mimi, her face full of relief. They'd managed to avoid having their cover blown once again, but the space camp would be finished in two days and Cindy would expect them to go back to England. Leah tried to push the thoughts of what might happen if they couldn't get the watch to send them back home by then from her mind. She just had to hope that their reason for being at the NACA would become clear soon.

They made the trek across to the West Computing Area, passing the big car park outside the Aeronautics building. Cindy searched for her mum's car and found it parked in its normal spot. Inside the West Computing building, the corridors were already busy with human computers rushing to and fro, their arms full of important-looking documents. Cindy weaved her way around them, waving occasionally and stopping to say hello. A couple of times she asked if they'd seen Nancy, but no one had.

Eventually, they arrived at the main computing room. Most of the women were sat at desks, heads bent over their calculators. There was a quiet, studious air to the room, and the concentration was so thick, Leah felt like she could reach out and touch it.

Nancy's desk was empty, so Cindy made a beeline for the one next to it. A woman with large gold earrings sat there.

'Excuse me, Dolly, have you seen my mom anywhere today?' Cindy asked politely.

Dolly smiled gently and shook her head. 'I'm sorry, dear, but I haven't.'

'Okay, thank you,' Cindy said, turning away. A small frown pinched the space between her eyebrows.

'What's wrong?' Leah asked as Cindy's eyes roamed over her mother's desk.

'Something feels strange,' Cindy replied. 'We haven't seen Mom since last night and no one has seen her today. There isn't even a cup of coffee on her desk and she *always* has a coffee in the morning.'

'What are you saying?' Mimi asked slowly. 'Do you think something's happened to her?'

Cindy bit her lip. She scooped Marty out of her dress and held him close to her chest, stroking a fingertip down his back. 'I don't know. But I *do* know that this isn't like her.'

'I'm sure there's a reasonable explanation. After all, her car's here,' Leah pointed out. 'Maybe she got called away to work in another building?'

'Maybe,' Cindy said thoughtfully, but then she shook her head. 'If that were the case, though, someone would know about it.'

'Well,' Mimi said. 'There's only one way to find out for sure if anyone has seen her.' She stepped forward and cleared her throat.

'Meems, what are you doing?' Leah hissed, but Mimi ignored her.

'Excuse me? Excuse me!' Mimi shouted. The women all looked up, their faces full of confusion. 'I'm really sorry to disturb you, but we're just wondering, has anyone seen Nancy?'

The human computers frowned and stared at each other. A few shook their heads, but no one spoke.

Leah glanced over at Cindy. Her bottom lip was trembling slightly and her hands were clasped tightly around Marty. Her dark eyes gleamed.

'What's going on in here?' boomed a familiar voice.

Immediately, the women rose from their desks, like soldiers standing to attention. Leah turned to see that Mr Whistler was stood in the doorway.

Mr Jones and Miss Sinclair were standing behind him.

The director of the NACA held up his hand and gestured for the women to sit. 'There's no need for that,' he said, stepping into the room. There was a collective shuffle and creak as everyone retook their seats. 'Although I would like to know what's got you so upset, Cindy.'

'Oh, Mr Whistler, sir, it's my mom! Her car is outside, but I can't find her anywhere!' A single tear dripped down Cindy's cheek.

Mr Jones snorted. Leah thought she heard him say, 'Ridiculous.'

But Mr Whistler ignored him. Instead, he crouched down so that he was on Cindy's level, a serious expression on his face. 'What do you mean?'

'She . . . she put us to bed and then she came back here to work. But when we woke up this morning, she wasn't there and now . . .' Cindy trailed off, took a deep breath, and then continued. 'Now I'm starting to wonder if she even came home at all last night.'

'She might have just got up early this morning, Cindy dear,' Miss Sinclair said kindly.

Cindy shook her head. 'No one's seen her,' she whispered.

'Hmm,' Mr Whistler rumbled. 'That is strange. But don't you worry, we'll get to the bottom of this.' He stood and turned to Mr Jones. 'Edward, contact Security and ask them to search the compound for Mrs Grant.'

Mr Jones's mouth flopped open. 'But . . . you can't be serious, sir? This is a huge waste of resources. She's just one woman, and there are plenty of other computers we can employ in her absence. This is completely—'

'Mr Jones!' Mr Whistler's voice was sharp with disapproval as he interrupted his lead engineer. 'I can't believe such heartless words have just come from your mouth. Nancy is a valuable member of our staff and now she could be *missing*. And even if that weren't the case, she's our best mathematician. Of course, there are other computers, but I like working with *her*. Now go and speak to Security!'

The room was deathly silent in the aftermath

of Mr Whistler's words. Mr Jones's face burned red. His gaze flickered to Leah and her friends and his eyes narrowed nastily.

'Yes, sir,' he said finally, before turning on his heel and marching away.

Mr Whistler sighed. 'I'm sorry about that,' he said. Then he placed a large hand on Cindy's shoulder. 'Don't you worry, though. We'll find your mother. Everything will be fine.'

Leah looked at Cindy. She didn't need to be a mind reader to guess what was going through her friend's head. She could see it plainly in the lines pinching Cindy's face.

Mr Whistler's Security might be able to find Nancy. But what would happen if they couldn't?

CHAPTER 10: CLUE DUST

'There's nothing you can do until we have more information.'

That's what Mr Whistler had said before he and Miss Sinclair had left. The personal assistant had lingered a moment to give Cindy a hug and then hurried after her boss. Now the four of them gathered round Nancy's desk, unsure what to do next. Leah clenched her fists at her side. She felt useless.

'Maybe we should go for a walk?' Mimi suggested. 'It might take your mind off things, Cindy.'

But Cindy shook her head, her cheeks shiny with tears. 'No, I can't leave. What if Mom comes back or Mr Whistler has some news? We should stay right here, just in case.'

Mimi blew out a breath, leaning back against the desk. She looked pleadingly at Leah, but Leah shrugged her shoulders. She didn't know what to do either.

One of the other computers called Cindy's name and beckoned her over. Cindy looked at Nancy's desk as if she couldn't even bear to be a few metres away from it, but in the end her manners won out, and she set off across the room. Since Mr Whistler had left, George had been strangely quiet, but as soon as Cindy was out of earshot, he came alive.

'Guys! This is it!' he said, his voice filled with excitement.

'This is what?' Mimi said, confused.

George rolled his eyes. 'This is why the watch brought us here!'

Leah stood up straighter as she considered George's words. She'd been so focused on Cindy and what this meant for her that she hadn't stopped to consider what it might mean for *them*.

'George!' Mimi gasped. 'You're a genius!'

'So, we just need to find Nancy and we'll be able to go home?' Leah asked excitedly.

'It makes sense, doesn't it?' George reasoned. 'Of course, if the watch wants *us* to find her, that means that Mr Whistler's Security aren't going to.'

Mimi's hands flew to her mouth dramatically. 'You mean . . . you think something bad has happened?'

George grimaced. 'I hope I'm wrong, but the watch never takes us back in time so that we can make friends and have a nice time, does it? Something *always* goes wrong.'

'We need to start investigating,' Leah said. She scanned Nancy's desk as if someone might have conveniently laid all the clues out for them.

'Do you think we should tell Cindy?' Mimi said hesitantly.

'Tell Cindy what?'

Leah whirled to see that Cindy was standing behind them, one eyebrow raised. Marty's head poked curiously from the top of her pocket.

Leah took a deep breath. 'Well . . .' she said.

'That we were just talking, and we were thinking that . . . maybe we should do some investigating of our own.'

Cindy shook her head. 'I told you. Mr Whistler—'

'I know,' Leah interrupted. 'But if we started to look for some clues about where your mum went, it could give us a head start if . . .' She trailed off, biting her lip. But Cindy already knew what she was going to say.

'If Mr Whistler doesn't find anything,' she said dully.

Leah nodded.

Cindy's face crumpled 'But we don't even know where to start! We'd never be able to find her on our own.'

'Cindy!' Mimi frowned at her. 'You can't think like that! I thought you wanted to be an engineer? Engineers don't run away from problems, they run *towards* them. It's their job to try to come up with as many solutions as they can. Isn't it?'

'I know, but . . .' Cindy began, her lip quivering. 'I don't know if I can do it without Mom here.

She helps me think of my best ideas.'

George stepped forward and rested his hand on Cindy's arm. 'We can help you. We'll work as a team to figure out what happened.'

Suddenly, a thought struck Leah. 'I know we don't have any clues yet,' she said slowly. 'But I have an idea about how we might find them.' She turned to Mimi and glanced meaningfully at her hoody pocket.

'Oh!' Mimi exclaimed. She looked at Cindy doubtfully. 'Are you sure, L? Last time—'

'It's our best bet,' Leah said.

'What are you talking about?' Cindy asked, her eyes shining with tears.

Determined, Leah held out her hand, and after a second, Mimi retrieved the magnifying glass and gave it to her. The lens winked in the light.

'What I'm about to tell you is going to sound ridiculous. But this –' she held up the magnifying glass, gripping its glossy wooden handle firmly – 'isn't just a magnifying glass. It's magic and it could help us find a hint about where your mum's disappeared to. It's a bit unreliable but—'

'How can you be so cruel?' Cindy hissed, interrupting her. 'My mom's missing and all you can do is tell stupid lies. This isn't a joke!'

'No, Cindy, she's not joking!' George exclaimed.

'It *is* magic!' Mimi cried at the same time.

Cindy scoffed and took a step back.

'Stop!' Leah shouted. A few of the human computers looked up to see what the noise was

and she lowered her voice. 'Just . . . just stop and listen.'

Cindy stared at her coldly.

Leah sighed. 'I understand why you don't believe us. But I promise I'm not making this up. I'll show you.'

Hoping that the magnifying glass wouldn't let her down, Leah turned to Nancy's desk, lifted the glass to her eye and looked through it.

All she saw was a blurry close-up of Nancy's papers and her clunky calculator. There wasn't any golden clue dust in sight.

'Is it working?' Mimi asked eagerly. 'Can you see anything?'

Leah's mouth twisted in frustration. She couldn't understand why the magnifying glass didn't work when she needed it to. She thought back to when they'd been stranded in the rainforest, searching for Mwamba, the baby chimpanzee. She remembered begging the magnifying glass to show her *something*.

She did the same now. She thought about Nancy, and how kind she'd been to them at the diner the night before. She thought about Cindy and how upset she was about her mum's disappearance. *Please*, she thought to the magnifying glass, *please help us.*

Leah gasped as she watched a trail of sparkling clue dust erupt through the lens of the magnifying glass like sunlight twinkling on the ocean waves. It highlighted a path which curled out of the doorway and into the corridor. She grinned broadly and turned to Cindy.

'If you don't believe me, why don't you see for yourself?' she asked, holding the magnifying glass out.

Cindy took it cautiously. She lifted it to her face and inhaled sharply as she saw the golden dust.

'Holy mackerel, what *is* that?' she exclaimed.

'That,' George said smugly, 'is clue dust.'

'And we should really follow it before it decides it's had enough and disappears,' Mimi said. 'Leah, why don't you lead the way?'

Stunned, Cindy gave the magnifying glass back to Leah.

'Okay, this way!' Leah said. She set off into the corridor, the others following behind her.

The clue dust branched off in a glittery pathway across the NACA compound. It twisted around buildings and down staircases, threading its way around dustbins and bushes. The children followed it in a breathless line. Leah couldn't believe the magnifying glass had worked when she asked it to, and curiosity urged her feet to move faster as she thought about what they might find at the end of the trail.

It came to a stop at the car park outside of the Aeronautics building, the clue dust dissolving into thin air like pollen specks carried away on the wind.

Leah let the magnifying glass drop to her side, staring around her. There was nothing there.

'I don't understand,' she said, shaking her head. 'Why has it brought us here?'

George scanned the ground. 'There has to be a reason!'

'I don't know why you're surprised,' Mimi said, shaking her head bitterly. 'That thing can never make its mind up about whether it wants to help us or not.'

Cindy wrapped her arms around herself tightly but said nothing. Marty clambered up to her shoulder and nosed her cheek in comfort.

Leah bit her lip. This didn't make sense. Yes, the magnifying glass was unreliable, but it had never been *wrong* before. If it had brought them here, there had to be a reason for it. She looked up, scanning the rows of parked cars.

'Wait,' she said suddenly, her eyes snagging on something in the distance. 'Who are *they*?'

She pointed towards the back of the car park where two figures were leaning against a black car. Leah could tell they were both wearing suits, but they were too far away to make out any other details.

Mimi squinted. 'Did we see them yesterday?'

Leah shook her head, but before she could ask Cindy if the men were familiar, a voice spoke.

'Ah, children. You're here.'

Leah spun round to see that Mr Whistler was coming down the steps from the Aeronautics building with Miss Sinclair trailing behind. At the bottom, Apollo, the security guard's dog, thumped his tail, and she stopped to stroke him fondly.

Cindy stepped forward eagerly. 'Did Security find my mom?' Her voice was full of hope.

Mr Whistler's face was grave, the lines around his mouth deeper than they had been earlier.

'I'm so sorry, Cindy . . .' he began.

'No!' Cindy gasped.

'We can't find any trace of your mother. We've contacted the police and they'll be here shortly to take statements.'

Cindy moaned, covering her eyes. Her shoulders shuddered and Leah stepped forward, putting an arm around her.

'What do we do now?' she said.

'We wait,' Mr Whistler said regretfully. 'I'll do everything I can to support the police investigation, but . . . we must be prepared for the worst. I'm worried that perhaps this is a Soviet plot.' At his words, Cindy sobbed.

'What do you mean?' George asked.

'I mean that Nancy Grant is our best mathematician. If the Soviet Union wanted information on our space programme, she would be one of the key people to target.' Mr Whistler paused as though he didn't want to say the next words. 'If I'm right, and Nancy has been kidnapped by the Soviet Union . . . well, I'm afraid there's not a lot any of us can do.'

CHAPTER 11: INTERROGATIONS AND INTERVIEWS

It took a long time after Miss Sinclair and Mr Whistler had left for Cindy to calm down. Her sobs rang out, despite Leah's and her friends' attempts to comfort her, as they sat together on the steps of the Aeronautics building.

Leah couldn't even imagine how Cindy must be feeling. She didn't know what she'd do if her own mum had gone missing. Even the thought made her shudder. Finally, Cindy stopped crying and stared out over the car park, her eyes red and swollen.

'Do you want to go home?' Leah asked her gently, but Cindy shook her head.

'No. I'd only have to sit and listen to Gramma panic too,' she said. 'I just . . . I can't believe it.

Mom's been kidnapped just for being clever. How is that fair?'

'It isn't,' Mimi said, frowning.

'Don't the Soviet Union have their own mathematicians?' Cindy's voice was thick with despair, and she buried her head in her hands once more.

At the mention of the Soviet Union, Leah suddenly remembered the mysterious figures they'd seen before Mr Whistler had arrived. She straightened, craning her neck to see over the cars, but they'd vanished. Leah frowned.

'Those strange people we saw,' she said slowly. 'You don't think they had anything to do with it, do you?'

Cindy's head popped up. 'I bet they did!' she said angrily. She clambered to her feet. 'Where are they? I'm going to go up to them and . . .' She broke off as she scanned the car park and realized that they were no longer there.

'Hang on, Cindy,' George said, jumping up to stand next to her. 'We need to be careful!'

'Well, I'm not just going to wait around for

the police,' Cindy told them, hands on her hips. 'They can't be trusted anyway. If a white person had gone missing, that would be one thing. But everyone knows they don't care when it happens to Black women. Besides, if there are Soviet agents hanging around, I'm not letting them get away. I'm going to find them!'

'And we'll help you,' Mimi said, taking Cindy's hand. 'But George is right. We need some kind of plan.'

'Can't you just get that magic glass thing out again?' Cindy demanded.

Leah shook her head regretfully. 'I wish I could, but it doesn't work like that. The magnifying glass has taken us to where it thinks we need to be. Now the rest is on us.'

'So what do we do next?' Cindy cried.

'Well,' Mimi said. 'If the Soviet Union *did* kidnap your mum, they must have had help to know where she'd be. We need to work out who might have been working with them. Let's create a list of suspects!'

Cindy looked faintly impressed. 'That's a swell

idea. How did you think of that?'

Mimi smiled, looking pleased with herself. 'I watch a lot of detective films.'

'Who has a reason not to like your mum, Cindy?' Leah said, and Cindy's brow furrowed in thought.

'Well, there are plenty of people at the NACA who would rather the human computers didn't exist, particularly those in the West Computing Area. They don't like that women are in charge of so much important math, especially women who aren't white. I mean, Mr Jones, for starters. He's had it in for my mom since day one!'

'And remember what he said to her yesterday?' George piped up. 'He told her that she had to find a solution or who knew what would happen to her next.'

'Oh yeah! That is suspicious! He's basically admitted to it,' Mimi said excitedly, but then she wilted like a flower. 'That won't be enough, though. We need to find evidence to prove that he's guilty so everyone will believe us when we accuse him.'

'How are we going to do that?' Cindy asked. From her pocket, Marty squeaked as if he, too, were wondering the same thing.

Mimi grinned. 'That's the fun part. We need to be proper detectives.'

Leah nodded. 'We'll have to conduct interviews.'

Now that she had a purpose, Cindy seemed more composed. There were no more tears as she led Leah, Mimi and George back to the West Computing Area, where they were going to start their interviews.

They spoke to a few of the human computers first. They had agreed that Mimi had the best stage presence, so she asked the questions, whilst George wrote the answers down using a pen and notepad that they'd swiped from Nancy's desk. Leah and Cindy listened carefully to the answers, searching for any clues.

'When did you last see Nancy Grant? . . . Was there anything unusual about her behaviour? . . . What happened next?'

The human computers all answered dutifully.

'Nancy?' one of the women replied. 'Why, she was here last night. I saw her at her desk around eight o'clock.'

'Now that I think about it,' another woman said, 'she did seem a little out of sorts. She was shuffling some papers around and huffing a bit. Although . . . we all feel like that at the moment. Those engineers are working us to the bone and there's not enough of us to get everything done! Anyway, I didn't want to interrupt her.'

The final person they spoke to was a stout woman who looked twice Nancy's age. 'You want to know what happened next?' she said. 'Well, she left. At about half past eight. She gathered all her papers together and stormed out. I think she went to the Aeronautics building, but she didn't come back. I was the last one here and I left at half past ten. Locked the door up behind me.'

After they had questioned everyone they could at the West Computing Area, Leah, Mimi, George and Cindy rushed back over to the Aeronautics building. They had planned to interrogate Mr Jones next, but he wasn't in his office. They finally hunted him down in the cafeteria, eating a sandwich, but when Mimi asked to speak to him, he looked down his long nose and scowled.

'I don't have time to waste on silly little children who shouldn't even be here,' he spat. Then, before Mimi could say anything else, he gathered his lunch and marched away.

In the notebook, under Mr Jones's name, George wrote the words 'NO COMMENT'.

'Well, if Mr Jones won't talk, who do we interview next?' Mimi rubbed her chin in thought, but Cindy brightened.

'We need someone who works closely with him, but not too closely that they won't give us the information we need.' She smiled broadly. 'And I know just the person.'

Miss Sinclair's desk was located right outside Mr Whistler's office, which was at the end of a long room filled with busy engineers. Leah and her friends navigated their way through, smiling uncomfortably when anyone looked their way.

'This is a bad idea,' George whispered as a man with bushy eyebrows gave them a particularly angry glare. 'We're going to get thrown out.'

'Stop panicking,' Cindy replied. She walked with her back straight and her chin tipped up. 'My mom told me that the surest way to fit in somewhere is to act like you already belong. So that's what we have to do.'

Self-consciously, Leah uncurled her shoulders and mimicked Cindy's posture. After a few seconds, she realized that she was attracting far fewer curious glances. It really worked!

Still, she was relieved when they reached Miss

Sinclair's desk. Mr Whistler's personal assistant was tapping furiously on a typewriter, humming what sounded like the American national anthem under her breath. On the wall behind her was an enormous American flag, proudly pinned next to a filing cabinet which had a photograph of President Eisenhower stuck on the front. Her desk was bare, except for a coffee-filled mug, with another American flag on it, and a small badge in the shape of a shield. In the middle was a white number eleven.

Miss Sinclair looked up as Leah and her friends approached her desk. There were deep bruise-like smudges beneath her eyes and Leah thought she looked tired. Her gaze dipped to Cindy's pocket, and Miss Sinclair gave a squeak, scraping her chair backwards and pointing a trembling finger. 'Cindy! What on earth is that?'

Cindy looked down, confused, but then she brightened. 'Oh! This is Marty. My mouse.'

'A . . . a mouse? Here?' Miss Sinclair shuddered and closed her eyes briefly. 'You can't bring it in here! No, no, stay there! Don't get it anywhere near me.'

Cindy had taken a step towards the desk, fishing Marty from her pocket and holding him in her clasped palms. At Miss Sinclair's exclamation, she stopped.

'Are you scared of mice?' Leah asked, tilting her head to the side. Marty was so tiny, Leah couldn't understand how anyone could find him frightening.

Miss Sinclair shook her head quickly. 'No, no, of course not! Me, scared of that little thing?

Don't be silly. Mr Whistler is far more afraid of them than me! I just think animals don't belong in the workplace. That's all.' She forced a chuckle, but didn't take her eyes off Marty. When Cindy slipped him back into her pocket, Miss Sinclair visibly relaxed. 'Now, what do you four need?'

Cindy took a breath. 'We know that Mr Whistler is doing everything he can to find my mom, but if it's okay, we'd like to ask you some questions.'

'Oh, um, I . . .' Miss Sinclair mumbled.

'It'll only take a moment.' Cindy sighed theatrically, and Leah thought that she was almost as good an actress as Mimi. 'I just want to make sure that I haven't missed anything important.'

Miss Sinclair's face melted with compassion and she leaned forward to grip Cindy's hand tightly across the desk. 'Oh, you poor cherub. Of course I can answer a couple of your questions. Nancy is my good friend, you know. I'm sick with worry for her.'

'Great!' Mimi jumped in. 'Firstly, could you tell us if you saw Nancy at all last night?'

'I'm afraid I didn't,' Miss Sinclair replied, shaking her head reluctantly. 'I left early, at about half past five.'

Leah exchanged a dismayed look with Cindy. Miss Sinclair was their best shot at getting some evidence against Mr Jones. If she hadn't even been on the compound when Nancy went missing, this was a waste of their time.

Mimi wasn't ready to give up, though. 'When we met you yesterday afternoon, you were trying to stop Nancy and Mr Jones fighting. Do they disagree often?'

Miss Sinclair gave a giggle, as if that were a silly question. 'Do they ever!' she said. 'Cindy here could have told you that. Those two are always at odds.'

'But why? What's the problem?' Mimi pressed.

For a moment, Miss Sinclair looked uncomfortable, but then her expression smoothed over, and Leah wondered whether she'd imagined seeing anything else but her soft smile. 'Well, it's complicated, but let's just say that our Mr Jones has some authority issues, which means he doesn't like people telling him what to do. And dear Nancy – she isn't afraid to speak her mind. That, added to all of the jealousy . . . it's not a surprise they aren't the best of friends.'

'Jealousy?' Leah asked. 'What do you mean?'

'Oh dear.' Miss Sinclair covered her mouth with a hand. 'Perhaps I shouldn't have said that.'

'Said what? Oh please, tell us! It could be important!' Cindy pleaded.

Miss Sinclair hesitated a moment, but then she looked around to make sure that no one was listening. 'The fact of the matter is that Mr Jones is just plain jealous of Nancy,' she said in a low voice. 'Mr Whistler trusts her, and Mr Jones doesn't like that. Besides, I don't think he likes that someone like her is so high up in the space programme.'

'Someone like her?' Leah prompted, and Miss Sinclair nodded.

'You know. A woman. He thinks science is a man's job and that us women should all just run home to our children. Add to that the fact that Nancy isn't white . . . well, Mr Jones just doesn't believe she has a place in these offices. Or any offices at all.' Miss Sinclair's lips thinned into a disapproving line.

Indignation welled in Leah's chest, and she was suddenly furious. Before she could say anything, though, the door behind Miss Sinclair banged open. Mr Whistler appeared, a folder clutched in his hand. The PA stood so suddenly that her chair nearly toppled backward.

Mr Whistler frowned when he saw Leah and her friends. His gaze swung between them and his personal assistant.

'Children, what are you doing in here? This is a place of important work. My engineers can't afford to be distracted,' he said sternly.

Cindy stepped forward, looking sheepish. 'I'm sorry, Mr Whistler. It's my fault. I wanted to do something to help find my mom, so Miss Sinclair was helping by answering some questions—'

Mr Whistler shook his head and gave a loud sigh, interrupting her. Leah almost felt herself shrinking beneath the weight of his obvious disapproval.

'Cindy,' he said wearily. 'I know you want to help, but right now, all you're doing is getting in the way. What I need is for the four of you to let the authorities do their job. Can you do that for me?'

'Yes, Mr Whistler, sir,' said Cindy in a small voice.

'Good,' he said with a smile. Then he turned to his PA as if the children were no longer there. 'Miss Sinclair, where are those reports? I needed them two hours ago. And get me Mike on the phone. Quickly!'

He turned to leave and the phone on Miss Sinclair's desk rang. She picked it up.

'Hello, Mr Whistler's office, how can I help? Oh! Oh my, yes, sir. One moment please.' She leaned forward, pressing the phone to her chest. 'Mr Whistler, I'm sorry, but—'

'Don't be sorry, Miss Sinclair, just be faster,' Mr Whistler said, his voice thick with impatience. 'What is it?'

'It's the President, sir. And I'm not sure he sounds very happy.' Miss Sinclair seemed to shrink away from the director.

But Mr Whistler only sighed. He rubbed a hand over his forehead. 'Of course he would choose to ring now,' he muttered half to himself. And then, louder, he said, 'Patch him through and make sure I'm not interrupted. And you four . . .' He spun back to Leah and her friends. 'Stay out of the way, please.'

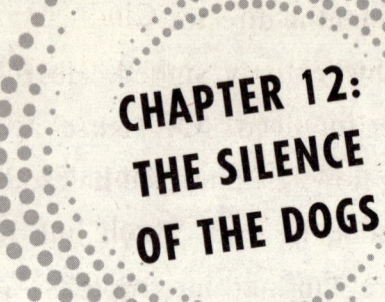

CHAPTER 12: THE SILENCE OF THE DOGS

'What are we supposed to do now?' Cindy snapped as they marched through the lobby of the Aeronautics building. 'We can't carry on with the interviews – if Mr Whistler finds out, we'll be in *big* trouble.'

George flicked through his notepad. 'We got some good stuff, though,' he said.

'Like what?' Cindy snorted. 'All we really know is that Mr Jones doesn't want to talk to us, and that Miss Sinclair is scared of Marty.'

'That's not true,' Leah argued. 'We know that your mum was upset about something when she left the West Computing Area last night.'

'*And*,' said Mimi, holding up a finger, 'we know what time she left.'

'How does that help us?' Cindy demanded. The further they got from Mr Whistler's office, the more her thunderous expression dissolved into one of sadness and disappointment.

'Conducting interviews is only one part of investigating a crime,' Mimi explained. 'All the best detectives on TV make sure they also have a good understanding of the timeline of events. If we want to figure out what happened to your mum, Cindy, we need to know exactly where she was at different times so we can track her movements. Then we might be able to find out who else was there.'

Cindy's face lit up with understanding. 'Wow, Mimi, you're pretty good at this!'

George chuckled. 'What she's good at is watching TV.'

'Well, you're lucky I am!' Mimi replied with a grin. 'Now, is there anywhere around here that tracks the employees when they come in and out?'

'We could check the punch-in sheet,' Cindy suggested. 'It's where the employees sign in and out so that the people in charge can make sure they're working the right hours.' She pointed to the reception desk at the front of the foyer. Bert, the security guard, was sitting behind it. 'There should be one for the Aeronautics building over there.'

'What about the West Computing Area?' Leah asked, but Cindy shook her head.

'My mom's building doesn't have one,' she said, biting her lip. 'I'm not sure the board thinks the human computers are important enough for that.'

'Oh well.' Leah sighed, trying not to feel frustrated. 'Let's see what the sheet for this building can tell us, at least. Mr Jones does work here, after all, so it might help us form a picture of what he was doing last night.'

Bert watched them approach the desk, his blue eyes tracking their movements carefully. He was chewing a piece of gum loudly, and as his mouth moved, Leah could see a gold tooth glinting amongst his molars.

'Can I help ya, kids?' His voice was warm and friendly.

'Afternoon, Bert,' Cindy said politely. 'We just

wondered if we could check the punch-in sheet for yesterday.'

The security guard narrowed his eyes. 'And why would ya want to do that?'

'Miss Sinclair sent us,' Mimi replied immediately. 'She wasn't sure if she signed in yesterday morning, so she asked us to check before Mr Whistler sees.'

Mimi's invented excuse must have been good enough for Bert, because he only shrugged. 'Sure ya can,' he said, leaning down and opening a drawer. He took out a clipboard and flipped a few pages over before he handed it across the desk. 'Don't be going anywhere with that, though. I need it for my records.'

Cindy promised she wouldn't, and then the four of them huddled over the paper. There was a table printed on it, with six columns: *Date*, *Name*, *Occupation*, *Time In*, *Time Out* and *Signature*. It didn't take Leah long to find Mr Jones. His name was printed in big, blocky letters.

'Here,' she said. 'Look. He left at nine o'clock last night.'

Cindy suddenly gasped and pointed to a name further down, written in elegant, cursive script: *Nancy Grant*. 'Mom was here!'

'What time?' Mimi asked, peering forward.

'It looks like she arrived at eight fifty,' Leah said, squinting to make sure she was reading the numbers right. 'But there's no sign-out time. She never left.'

'That can't be right.' Cindy shook her head, her expression stricken.

'It would explain why her car is still here, though,' George reasoned.

'But if she never left, where is she?' Cindy argued. 'Mr Whistler couldn't find her.'

'Okay, let me make sure I've got this right,' Mimi said. She held up her fingers, ticking each one off as she spoke. 'Nancy arrived at the West Computing Area after she put us to bed at roughly eight p.m. At eight thirty, she left with some papers, seeming upset. She came over here and signed in at eight fifty. Then Mr Jones left at nine, but Nancy didn't leave at all. And now, no one can find her.'

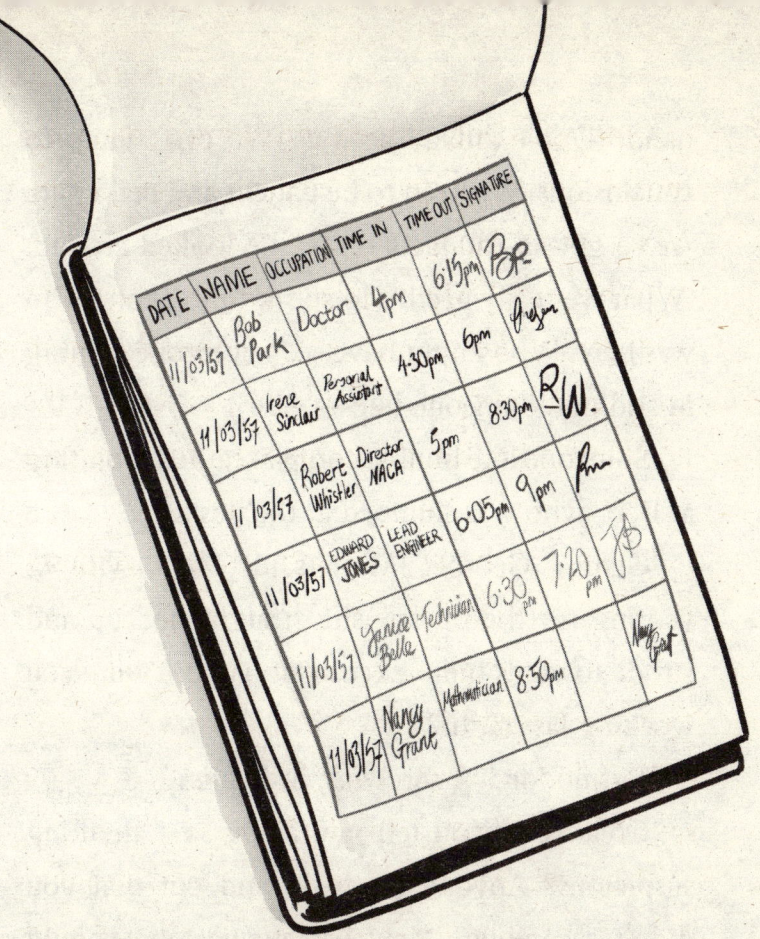

'Who else was in the building?' Leah asked.

George scanned the sheet again and shook his head. 'No one,' he said. 'Miss Sinclair left before six and Mr Whistler was gone by eight thirty.'

'What if . . .' Cindy's voice trembled. 'What if Mr Jones did something to hurt her?'

Leah reached forward and gripped Cindy's

hand. 'Don't think like that. We can't jump to conclusions. We need to be patient and make sure we've got all the facts first.' She looked around. 'What we really need is to speak to someone who was here. Who might have seen everyone coming in and out. Someone like—'

'Someone like him!' George breathed, pointing at Bert, who was slumped at the desk.

'Genius, George!' Mimi said. Then, without waiting for the others, she straightened up and strode towards him. 'Excuse me, sir, but were you working last night?'

Bert nodded. 'I sure was, little miss.'

'Great. Can you tell me if you saw anything suspicious? Anyone going in and out that you didn't recognize? Maybe someone who should have left but didn't?'

The security guard looked at them suspiciously. 'This is about that Mrs Grant, isn't it?' He shook his head. 'I already told the police everything I know!'

'Oh, please, Bert,' Cindy begged, coming to stand by Mimi. 'She's my mom. I just want to know what happened.'

Bert stared at them and then heaved a sigh. 'Mrs Grant left the building at about nine fifteen. I remember because I told her she had to sign out. She told me she wouldn't be long. She just needed to get some more documents from her desk. But then she never came back.'

Leah and her friends looked at each other. So Nancy *had* left the building.

'And did anyone go after her?' Mimi probed, but the security guard shook his head.

'No one. Mr Jones signed out just before her and before him was Mr Whistler. I saw him get into that junk-heap of a car he drives . . .' The security guard suddenly closed his mouth with a snap. He looked around as though checking to make sure no one had overhead him. 'Not that there's anything wrong with his car. I guess these fancy scientists have better things to worry about than motors, and I heard he's too busy with his work to bother about fixing one up—'

'What about Mr Jones?' Leah said, interrupting him. 'Did he get into his car, too?'

'He doesn't have one,' Bert said. 'He gets the bus.'

Leah sighed. She wasn't sure if any of this information was helpful, but she forced a smile anyway. 'Thank you,' she said, and then, after handing the sign-in sheet back, she and her friends headed out of the glass doors and down the stairs towards the car park.

'We're never going to find her, are we?' Cindy said in a small voice. 'All of these clues and investigations . . . we're running around in circles. Even your magic magnifying glass couldn't help us.'

Leah looked down at her feet, guilt surging through her. She'd been so sure the magnifying glass would help, but all she'd actually done was give Cindy false hope.

'Wait,' George suddenly said, stopping with one foot hovering over the final step. His eyes were wide behind his glasses as they roamed over the parked cars. 'What if . . . what if the magnifying glass wasn't wrong? What if we just didn't understand what it was trying to tell us?'

'George, what are you on about?' Mimi said, irritated.

George turned to look at them, his face full of excitement. 'It all makes sense! Nancy left the Aeronautics building to go to the West Computing Area, but she never came back. And the magnifying glass brought us right here. What if that's because this is where Nancy went missing?' He pointed emphatically at the pavement beneath their feet.

'You think she got lost in a car park?' Mimi raised her eyebrow.

'No,' Leah said, excitement brightening her eyes. 'That's not what he means. He's saying . . . what if the reason no one can find Nancy on the compound is because she's not here any more? She would have had to cross the car park to get to the West Computing Area, but we know she never made it. What if she got in someone's car and they drove her away with no one realizing?'

Cindy gasped. 'But then . . . she could be anywhere and anyone could have her!'

'That's not true, though,' Mimi said slowly.

She was looking at Apollo, who was sleeping with his large head resting on his golden paws. 'Because *he* would have stopped them.'

Suddenly, Mimi turned and sprinted back up the stairs and into the Aeronautics building.

'Mimi, wait!' Leah called, but Mimi was already through the doors and in front of the reception desk. Leah watched as Bert leaned towards her. He shook his head and said something. Mimi nodded, and then turned, pushing back through the doors and standing at the top of the steps. Her face was glowing with triumph.

'It can't have been just anyone, Cindy,' she said. 'You told us that Apollo barks at strangers until he gets to know them. The security guard said that Apollo didn't make a peep all night, which means . . .'

'Apollo knew whoever took your mum! It wasn't a stranger!' Leah breathed, the realization flooding over her like a plume of ice-cold water. 'And that means that Nancy probably knew them too.'

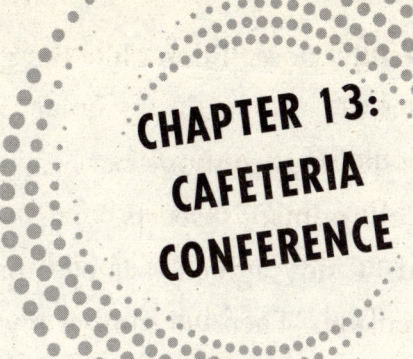

CHAPTER 13: CAFETERIA CONFERENCE

The cafeteria next to the West Computing Area was loud with chatter and busy with bodies when Leah and her friends arrived, but they managed to snag seats at the end of a half-empty table. Cindy pulled the sandwiches her gramma had made for them out of her bag and handed them out.

'There aren't any white people in here,' Mimi commented, looking round at the packed tables. 'Not like in the place Mr Jones was eating in.'

'That's because Black folks aren't allowed to eat in the same cafeterias as the white employees,' Cindy explained. She took a big bite of her sandwich.

Leah's mouth fell open. 'You can't be serious!'

'Sure I am. It's stupid, but those are the rules.'

Cindy wrinkled her nose. 'I don't like their stuffy cafeteria anyway.'

Mimi frowned, but then shook her head. 'Shall we look over our primary suspects?'

'We should,' Cindy agreed, her eyes blazing with a renewed fire. 'Then we can get my mom back.'

'Which one should we start with?' George said, picking at his food.

'There's only one, isn't there?' Mimi said. 'Mr Jones! There's no one else who was around late last night, and no one with a motive as strong as his. You heard Miss Sinclair. He was jealous of Nancy and he didn't like that Mr Whistler relied on a woman so much to make important decisions. It's got to be him!'

Leah shook her head. 'You're probably right, but we have to look at all our options. We can't jump to conclusions, Meems.'

Suddenly, the noise in the cafeteria dimmed, like someone had turned the volume down. Leah looked up and saw that most of the human computers were staring towards the door, where

Miss Sinclair was standing.

'Sorry to interrupt your lunch, ladies,' she said, in a punctual voice that didn't sound sorry at all. 'But Mr Whistler has requested a new computer to come over and help the engineers whilst Nancy... well, whilst our previous computer is on leave.'

At this, one of the women at the other end of the children's table snorted quietly. It was Dolly, the woman with the big gold earrings whose desk was next to Nancy's.

'We'll send someone over this afternoon, Mrs Sinclair,' Dolly said after a brief pause. 'Once we've all had something to eat.'

'Of course,' Miss Sinclair said, a faint blush staining her cheeks. 'Thank you, Dorothy.' Her eyes darted to Leah and her friends, and she gave them a quick wave before leaving.

'Eeesh,' Dolly said to the person opposite her. 'As if we don't have enough work to deal with as it is, now that we're understaffed.'

Her companion nodded in agreement, and then said in a low voice, 'Don't send me over there. That woman gives me the shivers.'

Leah frowned. Miss Sinclair had only ever been kind to her and her friends. Unable to help herself, she leaned forward.

'I'm sorry, I didn't mean to eavesdrop, but . . . don't you get along with Miss Sinclair?'

Dolly and her friend exchanged a look that Leah didn't fully understand. 'There's nothing wrong with her,' she said finally. 'It's just that she's so . . . committed to the space programme.'

'What does that mean?' Mimi said.

'Look, I'm as desperate to win this Space Race as everyone else is. I'm a proud American, after all. But I've got a life outside of the NACA. Miss Sinclair, on the other hand . . . I'm not so sure. She's fanatical about beating the Soviets.'

Leah thought back to the PA's desk, remembering the American flag stuck up on the wall, and her matching mug, along with the little American flag badges Miss Sinclair wore on her cardigan collar.

'You know . . .' Dolly's friend said, lowering her voice and looking around furtively, as if Miss Sinclair were about to pop out from underneath the table. 'I heard a rumour about her once. People say that she used to be part of an all-female astronaut programme, but then it was cancelled. That's why she decided to work for Mr Whistler. It's the closest she'll ever get to the stars.'

'That's so sad,' Leah said, her heart aching for Miss Sinclair's ruined dreams. 'Couldn't Mr Whistler make an exception for her?'

'Oh, honey,' Dolly said pityingly as she gathered her lunch tray and stood up. 'The men in charge don't make exceptions for women around here.'

As Dolly and her friend left, Leah thought about what she'd said. Could that be why Mr Jones had kidnapped Nancy? Maybe he was worried that Mr Whistler was relying on her too much and he was afraid Nancy might become more important than him.

It seemed that George's mind had also turned to their primary suspect, because he said, 'If Mr Jones did kidnap your mum, Cindy, where do you think he might have taken her?'

Cindy bit her lip in thought, and then she

shook her head. 'I don't know.'

'He must have left details of his plans *somewhere*,' Mimi said. 'Everyone around here seems to love taking notes.'

Suddenly, Cindy straightened, her eyes bright. 'You're right!' she breathed. 'Mr Jones is one of the most organized people working on the compound. He's even more organized than Mom and *that's* saying something. She once told me he likes to have a "paper trail".'

'What does that mean?' Mimi asked, making a face.

'It means that he won't have been able to resist writing all of his plans down. And I know exactly where he'll have stashed them.' Cindy looked at them triumphantly before announcing, 'His office!'

Leah slumped in her chair. 'That makes things more difficult, then,' she said, but Cindy was shaking her head.

'No, it doesn't.' She grinned. 'Let's break in!'

CHAPTER 14: LAIKA

Leah had never broken into anywhere before. Her entire body fizzed with anxiety as she tailed Cindy and her friends along the corridor.

'I don't think this a good idea,' said George, shaking his head. 'We're going to get caught. It's not too late for us to turn back. We could—'

Cindy whirled on him. 'We could what? Ask Mr Jones nicely to let us into his office so we can search through his desk for incriminating evidence? I don't think so, do you?'

George shrank beneath her glare. 'I just—'

'My mom is out there somewhere,' Cindy whispered forcefully. 'She's probably alone, and scared, and I need her back! The grown-ups won't help us and I don't trust the police. Mr Whistler has pretty much banned us from doing anything. But I can't just sit still. If there are documents in Mr Jones's office that will help my mom, then nothing is going to stop me from finding them. So, are you with me on this, or are you out?'

George held up his hands in surrender. 'I'm with you, I'm with you!'

'Don't worry, George,' Leah said. 'We'll be careful.'

But it seemed that there wasn't much reason for caution as they got closer to Mr Jones's office. The corridors swarmed with men and none of them were the slightest bit concerned with the children. They were all talking frantically, their expressions somewhere between excited and furious.

'What's going on?' Leah asked. At the end of the corridor, she saw the familiar form of Mr Whistler stomping away from them. His face was contorted with anger. Behind him came Miss Sinclair, her shoulders stooped and her face lowered. They vanished around a corner.

Something was wrong.

Cindy's face was pinched as she shook her head. 'I don't know. Come on, let's find out!'

They stopped in the open doorway of an office that was crammed with people. A radio was playing and Leah strained to hear what was being said. A man turned it up and the presenter's voice filled the small space.

'. . . *have had confirmation that the Soviet Union has successfully launched a living creature into orbit. Reports are coming in that the spacecraft, Sputnik Two, set off this morning containing a stray dog known as Laika* . . .'

The man who had adjusted the radio volume looked up. His eyes were glazed with bewilderment. 'They've done it. I can't believe . . .' He trailed off.

'We've lost?' said a secretary standing next to him. Leah saw her bottom lip tremble. 'Is the race over?'

'This can't be real,' Cindy said from her side. 'They *can't* have launched a dog into space. It's a joke. It has to be! We're winning, aren't we?' She looked at Leah for answers, but Leah just stared at her helplessly. Cindy's expression crumpled.

Leah didn't know what to do. She'd known that the Space Race was important to Cindy, but she hadn't realized how much until now. Now the devastation on her face proved that, for Cindy, beating the Soviet Union wasn't just a game. It meant *everything*. Sadness rocked through Leah. She didn't know much about science, but she did remember her history teacher telling her that the first person into space was a man called Yuri Gagarin, and Leah was pretty sure he hadn't been American. Leah had a feeling that Laika was just the beginning of Cindy's disappointments.

Still, she hated to see Cindy so upset.

'It's okay,' Leah said, wrapping her arm around her friend's shoulders. 'A dog isn't a person. There's still time for America to win!'

Mimi was too distracted to pay attention to what they were saying. She was staring at the radio sadly. 'That poor dog,' she said. 'I bet she was so frightened going up into space all on her own.'

'Don't you think it's a bit suspicious?' George

said thoughtfully, walking away from the office. 'That the Soviet Union have successfully launched a dog into orbit the day after your mum has gone missing?'

Cindy had been shuffling along, her eyes blank and unfocused. At the mention of Nancy, she jerked out of her trance. 'You're right! What if they kidnapped my mom because they've used her math to get ahead in the race?'

'Mr Jones must be a spy!' Mimi announced. 'I bet he's helping them from the inside!'

'But he's the lead engineer for the NACA,' Leah said, frowning.

Mimi shrugged. 'Maybe he doesn't care which side he's on, just so long as it's the one that wins. Maybe he's only doing all of this for the glory.'

'Well, there's only one way to find out, isn't there? We need to get into his office and get some evidence.' Leah looked up and down the still-busy corridor. Everyone was so engrossed in Laika that no one even spared them half a glance. 'And now, with everyone so distracted, it's the perfect time for a break-in.'

CHAPTER 15: THE KEY

Mr Jones's office was off the main corridor, so there weren't many people to witness Leah and her friends as they tried to carry out their break-in. They leaned against the wall next to his door until there was a pause in the traffic, and then, as soon as the coast was clear, Leah tried the handle. 'It's locked!' she groaned, although she wasn't surprised. Mr Jones struck her as the overly cautious type.

'Can you pick it?' Cindy asked. 'With a hairpin or something?'

Leah gaped at her. 'Where would I have learned to pick locks?'

Cindy shrugged. 'It was worth asking.'

'What are we going to do now?' George

moaned, his hands twisting together as he looked anxiously up and down the corridor. 'We're running out of time.'

'Let me try my screwdriver,' Cindy announced, plucking it from her pocket. She stuck her tongue out as she inserted it into the lock. It rattled around uselessly and Cindy frowned, taking it out. 'I suppose I could use it to take the whole lock off, but that would take some time and I'm *pretty* sure someone would notice.'

'Ugh,' Leah groaned. *Who decided it was a good idea to stage a break-in anyway?*

'Leah!' Mimi cried. 'The key!'

For a moment, Leah was confused. And then she remembered. After the watch had returned them from Tanzania, a new object had turned up in the box: a beautifully engraved silver key. In the panic of Nancy's disappearance, Leah had completely forgotten about it. They hadn't had a chance to try using it yet, but now was the perfect opportunity. What were keys for if not to open things?

George dug it out of his pocket. It was quite

large, nearly filling his whole palm. He looked uncertainly at the small keyhole set into Mr Jones's door.

'I don't think it's going to fit,' he said.

'Let me see,' Leah said, taking the key. Her stomach sank as she realized that George was right. The key was *far* too big.

'Is that another one of your magic objects?' Cindy asked, sliding her screwdriver back into her pocket. 'Like the magnifying glass?'

Leah nodded. 'I hope so, but we haven't actually used this one before. We're not sure what it does and these things are always a bit temperamental.'

'Well, you might as well try it out,' Cindy said, gesturing at the keyhole. She glanced up and down the corridor. 'And quickly, before someone turns up!'

Leah moved the key towards the lock. She gave it a little squeeze, just in case. *Please*, she thought, just like she had done with the magnifying glass. *We really need to get in here so we can find Cindy's mum and get home.*

The key seemed to shiver in her grasp, and

then Leah let out a little yelp as it began to *shrink*. It grew smaller and smaller, until it was the perfect size to fit into the lock on Mr Jones's door.

'No way!' Mimi breathed. 'That's so cool!'

'Where did you find all these magical objects?' Cindy gaped.

Leah didn't want to spend time they didn't have telling Cindy about the day they had discovered the watch, so she said nothing, inserting the key in the lock and turning it. It rotated with a satisfying clunk. Leah tried the door handle again, and grinned as it swung open before her.

'We're in!' she said, and then ushered the others inside. 'Quick!' She shut the door behind them.

Mr Jones's office was exactly as Leah had expected it would be. The walls were lined with bookshelves, the volumes arranged neatly in height order. A plain wooden door was slightly ajar in one corner, showing a storage cupboard with more shelves. A large pine desk and a chair sat in the middle of the room, its gleaming surface empty, except for a typewriter, an old-fashioned telephone and a pot filled with pens and sharpened pencils. On the back wall was a clean blackboard, the stubby fingers of chalk lined up neatly along the bottom like soldiers in a row. Next to the blackboard were three framed certificates. Leah peered up at them and blinked in surprise. They were for karate.

'We need to be fast if we're going to find anything to help my mom,' Cindy said. Her pocket wriggled and Marty poked out his nose. Cindy scooped him up and put him on the floor. 'Mr Jones might be distracted by the news, but he could be back at any minute.'

'What are we looking for?' George asked, moving towards one of the bookshelves.

'A folder or papers that mention my mom's disappearance, or a secret holding place,' replied Cindy. 'Maybe look for anything to do with the Soviet Union too. If Mr Jones is a spy, he must have some secret letters tucked away somewhere.'

The four of them got to work. George and Mimi started moving methodically around the bookshelves, whilst Cindy and Leah tackled the desk. There weren't any papers on top of it, but

once they'd pushed the chair out of the way, they could see a set of drawers and filing cabinets underneath.

Cindy tried to open one of them, but it wouldn't budge.

'Don't worry,' Leah said, brandishing the key. 'We have this!'

Once again, as Leah moved the key towards the lock on the drawers, she thought about how much she needed to see what was inside so they could help Nancy and get home. Her mum was always talking about doing things with *intention*. Leah didn't fully understand what that meant, but she thought it was about really meaning something when you tried to do it. And Leah *really meant* to get into those drawers.

But this time the key didn't shrink down to the right size. Instead, it sat still in her palm, refusing to even twitch.

Leah gritted her teeth. She should have known the key wouldn't help them out again so quickly.

Cindy, who'd been watching over her shoulder, groaned in frustration. 'What are we going to do now? We've got to get into those drawers!'

Leah slipped the key back in her pocket and frowned at the locked cabinets. 'There must be a spare key somewhere around here.'

'It could be anywhere,' Mimi said, exasperated.

There was a sudden high-pitched squeaking and Leah spun round to see that Marty had scampered over to the bottom shelf of the nearest bookcase. He was standing on his hind legs, his front paws braced against the spine of a red leather book. He squeaked again.

'What is it, boy?' George said, dropping to one knee next to the mouse. He moved Marty gently out of the way and pulled the red book off the shelf. He blinked in surprise when he saw there was a blue tab sticking out of the top, as if to mark it out from the rest of the books on the shelf. He let the book fall open and gasped when a small metallic shape dropped onto the carpet.

'A key!' Leah exclaimed. She turned to Cindy. 'How did he know that was in there?'

Cindy grinned as George handed the key over and replaced the book. 'Mice have an incredibly good sense of smell! He must have sniffed the metal out. Besides –' she leaned forward, her smile mischievous – 'I've always thought he was a little bit magic, like your key and your magnifying glass.'

Leah used the secret key to open all of the drawers, and Cindy began to slide them out, reaching inside to scoop up stacks of folders. After that, they worked mostly in silence. The only sound in the office was the shuffling of papers. Marty was still scampering around the room, sniffing in the corners as if searching for hidden treasure, but it seemed like there was none to be found. In fact, the more Leah searched, the more disappointed she became. Everything she read was about rockets, or science, or maths. There were a few letters from Mr Whistler, but they weren't very exciting and they didn't give them any clues about Nancy's disappearance. Besides, time was running out and Leah's insides churned as the minutes ticked by. Mr Jones could return at any moment!

Finally, Leah threw the last piece of paper

down with an exasperated sigh.

'Nothing!' she said and tipped her head back to look at George and Mimi. 'There's nothing here!'

'Just a load of boring books,' George said grumpily.

'What about you, Cindy?' Mimi called.

But Cindy didn't answer, because she was clutching a pile of papers, her eyes fixed on the top sheet.

'What is it?' Leah said, feeling a surge of excitement. 'Have you found something? Is it about your mum? The Soviet Union?'

Cindy shook her head. 'No, it's not that. It's . . . These are the numbers that Mr Jones said he gave my mom. The ones that caused the rocket to explode yesterday. But there's something wrong.'

'What do you mean?' Leah asked.

Cindy finally looked up. She was frowning. 'I mean they're incorrect. When I was at my mom's desk this morning, *her* calculations were there. I remember seeing them. But these numbers don't match the ones that she had. How can that be? Why are they different?'

Leah opened her mouth to answer, but before she could, she heard a familiar voice echoing down the corridor. Her blood ran cold.

'. . . Mr Whistler wants those papers now, Bob. We need to do something about this complete farce. Don't make him wait.'

It was Mr Jones.

CHAPTER 16: EAVESDROPPING

'Oh shoot!' Cindy hissed.

'I told you!' George whispered fiercely. 'Now what are we going to do?'

'We've got to tidy up before he gets here!' Mimi said, frantically collecting books.

Together, Cindy and Leah scrambled to stuff the papers back into the drawers, whilst George and Mimi shoved the books back onto the shelves. They'd made such a mess; there was no way they'd have time to clear it all up. Leah's heart was thumping as they heard Mr Jones's footsteps. George let out a whimper.

The door handle rattled. Leah realized they weren't going to make it. The door began to open and Leah stared in horror, waiting for him to appear – but then it paused as someone out in the corridor called Mr Jones's name.

'What is it?' Leah heard him say, irritated.

'Sorry to disturb you, sir,' the other person said. He sounded nervous. 'But I wanted to discuss my workload with you . . .'

Mr Jones huffed and said something in reply, but Leah wasn't listening. Heart hammering in her chest, she gestured at her friends. They resumed their frantic tidying, shoving papers and books away as fast as they could. Leah kept one eye on the door, but Mr Jones continued talking. When everything was back the way it had been, she juggled the key in her hands, reinserting it into each filing-cabinet drawer and securing it. Her fingers shook as she tried to race through them all.

'Look, Mike,' Mr Jones said suddenly from outside. He sounded very annoyed. 'I don't have time to listen to your snivelling. We're all under a lot of pressure, so just get on and do what you're paid to do or leave like the rest of your useless team! Now stop bothering me!'

There was no time. Throwing the last drawer shut and not bothering to lock it, Leah grabbed Cindy's arm and yanked her under the desk. Marty gave a squeak and scampered up her leg. Across the room, the door finally swung open as George and Mimi lunged for the storage cupboard, hiding in its shadowy depths just in time.

Mr Jones stepped inside, shutting the door firmly behind him.

Leah held her breath as he walked across to his desk, his shiny black shoes sinking into the spongey carpet. Next to her, Cindy squeezed her fingers hard, curling her legs up into her body. Leah prayed that the lead engineer wouldn't sit down at his desk. If he did, his knees would bump right into them. There was a muffled *thwump* and Leah guessed Mr Jones had dumped a stack of papers onto the desk. Then she heard a click and a rasping noise, like something being dragged round in a circle. There came a series of high-pitched beeps.

He was calling someone on the telephone.

'Get me Sam,' Mr Jones ordered, his tone like concrete. The person on the phone replied and Mr Jones tutted. 'I don't care if he's serving the President sweet tea, I need to speak to him now.' There was a pause. 'Ah, Sam, Mr Whistler asked me to call. We're bumping up the launch of Intrepid Two to tomorrow... Of course I saw the explosion yesterday, but it's all fine, we've fixed the math and there's nothing to worry about.'

From her hiding place, Leah could barely hear the voice on the other end of the phone, but it sounded panicked.

'Short-staffed?' Mr Jones continued. 'I don't give a hoot how many men you've got to drag out of bed! Do your job and make sure that rocket is on the launch pad tomorrow. The President wants results, so that's what we're going to give him. *Especially* after this morning.'

There was a bang as Mr Jones put the phone down.

Leah looked at Cindy, her eyes wide. Intrepid Two? Did Mr Jones mean there was another rocket? She thought back to the way the rocket had burst into flames yesterday. That must have been Intrepid One! But surely there was no way it was safe to do another launch so soon? Mr Jones had demanded that Nancy find a solution, and then she'd gone missing. Had he been lying when he'd told Sam the calculations had been fixed? The questions flew around Leah's head like shooting stars.

'Blasted ground personnel,' Mr Jones muttered from above. Then he bent his knees as if he were going to pull his chair forward and sit down. Leah swallowed a gasp and curled herself up as small as she could go. Her knee gave a twinge of pain, but Leah bit her lip, trying to ignore it. Cindy's eyes were round with alarm as they watched Mr Jones's legs.

Before Mr Jones could sit, though, something rolled off the desk and landed on the carpet, centimetres from Leah's foot. It was a pen. Mr Jones cursed and Leah sucked in a frightened breath as he began to bend down. Cindy clenched her eyes shut, squeezing Marty against her chest. As soon as Mr Jones reached down for his pen, the game would be up. He'd see them.

Suddenly, there was a bang on the office door and it swung wide.

'Edward?' came a male voice.

Mr Jones paused, and then straightened, standing upright and leaving the pen where it was. 'What do you want, Bob?'

'It's Mr Whistler,' Bob said. 'He wants to go

over the plans for the launch tomorrow.'

Mr Jones sighed. 'Of course he does. Come on then.'

He scooped the papers up from his desk and walked towards the door, his shiny shoes disappearing. The door banged shut.

Leah didn't move. She felt hot and cold at the same time and her vision swam, like she was dizzy. She stayed where she was, frozen beneath the desk. Next to her, Cindy was shaking, her eyes still shut as they waited to make sure Mr Jones was really gone. It wasn't until Mimi and George poked their heads out of the cupboard and called her name that she let herself relax.

Relief flooded through her, making her legs and arms feel like jelly. She huffed out a breath and rubbed a hand over her face. Cindy was breathing quickly and Marty let out a squeak of protest as she hugged him a little too hard.

Mimi's face appeared under the ledge of the desk and she extended her hand, pulling first Cindy and then Leah to her feet. Leah shook the ache out of her knee as she and her friends stared at each other, processing what had almost just happened.

'I thought for sure we were done for there,' Cindy said with a breathless chuckle.

George's eyes were wide and he was breathing shakily. 'C-come on,' he stuttered. 'Let's get out of here, before he comes back!'

Leah replaced the cabinet key in the red book and then the four of them crept to the door. Leah poked her head outside cautiously. She looked left and right to make sure the coast was clear before beckoning the others out. They shut the office door behind them.

'Did you hear what he said, though?' Mimi remarked as they strode down the corridor. Out of the four of them, she seemed the most composed. 'About the rocket launch?'

'I knew they'd built another Intrepid rocket, but they weren't supposed to be doing anything with it for months yet,' Cindy replied. Marty had clambered back into her pocket, and now his little head poked out of the top. 'Mom told me once that when a launch goes wrong, the engineers and scientists take their time analysing whatever mistakes were made and how they can prevent it from happening again.'

'Well, they're not taking their time now,' Leah said grimly. 'Your mum was right, Cindy. They're rushing, and letting their impatience get the better of them. I bet this whole thing with the Soviet rocket launch this morning has just made everything worse.'

George nodded. 'Mr Whistler needs to do another launch now so he can prove to the President that he can beat the Soviet Union.'

'But Mr Whistler wouldn't do that!' Cindy protested. She stopped and waved the papers she was holding. 'The numbers are clearly still not right, no matter what Mr Jones said. Mr Whistler would never do anything to risk anyone's safety.'

'Maybe Mr Whistler doesn't know that the numbers still don't match,' Leah said. 'On the phone, Mr Jones said the calculations had been fixed. But how do we know that's true? If he's willing to kidnap your mum to get what he wants, what's to stop him from lying to the NACA?'

'We need to head back to the West Computing Area and look at your mum's notes, Cindy,' Mimi said, determined. 'We need to figure out why the numbers are different.'

When they arrived at Nancy's desk, Leah was relieved to see that her papers were all still stacked in a pile. She'd been worried that the police might have taken them for evidence now that Cindy's mum was officially a missing person.

Cindy snatched the sheets up, her eyes moving rapidly across the page.

'What does it say?' George asked anxiously. 'Are they different?'

Cindy nodded. 'Completely. I don't understand how my mom would have got them this wrong. She's usually so thorough!'

'I guess everyone makes a mistake now and again,' Mimi said, shrugging her shoulders awkwardly.

'Or,' Leah said, frowning, 'someone *made sure* it was a mistake.'

'What do you mean?' Cindy asked.

'What if Mr Jones gave your mum the wrong numbers on purpose? What if he *wanted* the rocket to blow up and make her look bad?'

Cindy gasped. 'But that would be . . . that would be . . .' she spluttered, words failing her.

'Miss Sinclair did say that Mr Jones was really jealous of Nancy,' Mimi added, eyes wide. 'She said he didn't approve of her being a woman and having so much influence over Mr Whistler. But if she was found to be responsible for the rocket explosion . . .'

'Then Mr Whistler would have no choice but to get rid of her,' George finished.

Leah nodded. She knew how powerful jealousy could be. She'd felt it the other day, when she'd had to sit on the bench and watch her friends play whilst her injury had kept her on the sidelines. She'd have done anything then to magic her knee better so that she could get back on the pitch.

'Or maybe it doesn't have anything to do with my mom at all,' Cindy suggested. 'If Mr Jones really is a spy for the Soviet Union, exploding the rocket would mean that we wouldn't win the

Space Race.'

'And by giving her the wrong numbers, everyone would be blaming Nancy and not Mr Jones,' Leah agreed.

Cindy shook her head sadly. For a moment, Leah thought she might cry, but then she took a deep breath, pressing her lips together in determination. 'Either way, my mom is in danger. We *have* to go to Mr Whistler. He needs to know what we've found, and then he'll be able to have Mr Jones arrested. We'll finally find out what he's done with my mom.'

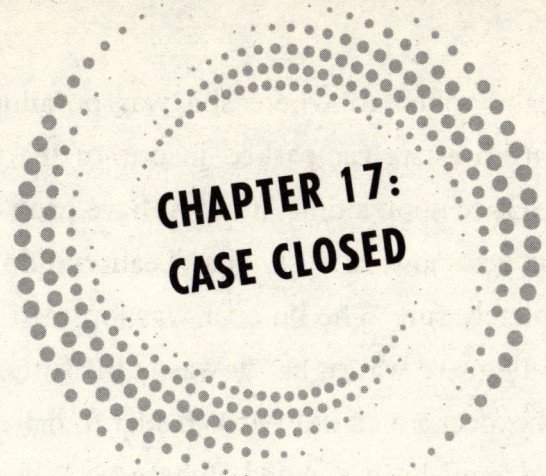

CHAPTER 17: CASE CLOSED

Leah, Mimi, George and Cindy raced across the compound. Cindy had the notes from her mum's desk and Mr Jones's office crushed in her fist. The afternoon was inching towards twilight and a dusky blanket was drawing itself over the sky, turning it from blue to a soft, bruised purple.

By the time they reached the Aeronautics building, they were all out of breath. Leah, especially, was struggling. Her knee was throbbing from all the back-and-forth. She didn't say anything to her friends, though. Instead, she gritted her teeth, rubbing the skin to try to ease the pain.

'I hope Mr Whistler's still here,' George panted.

'He is.' Cindy nodded. 'Look, there's his car.'

Leah looked to where she was pointing; at a beat-up estate car parked in one of the front bays. Once upon a time, it might have been blue, but it was now so rusty that Leah couldn't be completely sure. The bumper was lopsided. The security guard was right – it wasn't the sort of car she'd expect a man like Mr Whistler to drive.

Suddenly, Leah frowned. Behind Mr Whistler's car, towards the back of the car park, were the two strange figures she'd seen earlier. They were leaning against the bonnet of their shark-like car, staring towards the Aeronautics building.

Leah opened her mouth to point them out, but Cindy was already at the top of the steps.

'Come on!' she cried. 'Hurry up!'

Leah cast one more glance at the mysterious figures, and then followed her friends.

'Cindy, honey, come on now. Be reasonable!' Miss Sinclair said with a gentle smile. 'I can't just let y'all go storming in there. Mr Whistler is a very busy man.'

'But you don't understand,' Cindy pleaded.

'We've got vital evidence about my mom's disappearance, and Mr Whistler needs to know about it.'

The PA's smile faded, replaced with a slight frown. 'Now what did Mr Whistler say about interfering with this investigation? I hope you haven't been causing trouble for the police.'

'We haven't even *seen* any police,' Leah insisted. 'But we really do need to speak to Mr Whistler.'

Miss Sinclair shook her head. 'Look, you know I want the authorities to find Nancy just as much as you do, but I'm sorry, I can't let you in. Y'all are going to have to—'

'We don't have time for this!' Cindy interrupted. And then, so fast that Miss Sinclair couldn't stop her, she whirled and darted towards the door of Mr Whistler's office. The PA gave a cry as Cindy charged inside. She surged up from her desk, meaning to follow, but Mimi darted in front of her, stopping her from reaching the door. Leah rushed inside after Cindy.

The director of the NACA was on the phone. At first, he didn't see them, because he was standing up, his back to them, facing a large blackboard. His desk was orderly, with a few photo frames arranged on it. A stack of papers sat in the middle, on top of what looked like a map. There was a red circle highlighting a particular area, and Leah squinted, just able to make out the word 'Florida' printed within it.

'No, I'm telling you, the parts aren't the same. Intrepid One was an unfortunate accident!' The sharp snap of Mr Whistler's voice jerked Leah back to attention. It took her a second to realize that he wasn't talking to her but to whoever was on the phone. 'I don't have time to debate the specifics with you. After the Soviet launch earlier, the President wants results and we have to deliver or . . . well, you won't like the consequences. For *any* of us. I don't want to hear excuses! I can't help the budget cuts, and you *will* make it work.' Mr Whistler turned towards his desk and froze as he saw Leah and her friend. A strange expression crossed his face. 'Sam, I'm going to have to call you back.' He replaced the telephone on its stand, looking between them. His forehead was pinched in confusion, but his voice was kind as he said, 'Cindy. I'm surprised to see you here. What can I do for you?'

'Sir! I'm so sorry, sir!' Miss Sinclair finally barrelled into the room behind them, George and Mimi trailing behind her. Tendrils of mousy brown hair had escaped her bun. 'I tried to stop them but—'

Mr Whistler held up a hand. 'It's quite all right, Miss Sinclair. I'll deal with this. You can go on back to your desk.'

The PA shot the children one more flustered look before she left, leaving them alone with Mr Whistler.

'It's my mom,' Cindy said. Mr Whistler briefly closed his eyes in exasperation and opened his mouth to speak, but Cindy charged on before he could. 'I know you said not to get involved and we have been staying out of the way, I promise, but we found something that we think you should see.'

Mr Whistler raised an eyebrow. 'Oh?'

Cindy handed him the notes. 'We found these,

sir. Those ones on the left are Mr Jones's notes, and the other's are my mom's. As you can see, the numbers on them are completely different and we think . . .' She trailed off, looking at Leah, Mimi and George. Leah gave her an encouraging smile. 'Well, we think that Mr Jones gave my mom the wrong numbers on purpose. We think he was trying to make her look bad.'

'Or,' Mimi piped up, 'he's a Soviet spy.'

'Either way,' Leah added, 'we wanted to tell you because we heard that you're going to be launching another rocket tomorrow and we weren't sure if you knew that the calculations still weren't right.'

'How do you know about Intrepid Two?' Mr Whistler demanded, his expression hardening for a moment. Then he shook his head and held up a hand. 'Wait, no, it doesn't matter. What matters right now is that you've made some very serious accusations. And against my lead engineer, no less.'

Leah bit her lip. What if Mr Whistler didn't believe them?

But then he went on. 'However, these notes make for compelling reading.' He paused, running his eyes over the figures once more, and then sighed regretfully as he handed them back to Cindy. 'I can't ignore this. I fear you may be right. I'll have Mr Jones apprehended immediately.'

'What does that mean?' George whispered to Leah, but it was Mr Whistler who answered.

'It means that I'll call the police to arrest him.'

'And then they'll find my mom?' Cindy asked, almost vibrating at the thought.

Mr Whistler nodded. 'Yes, Cindy, I think we will.'

A smile bloomed across Cindy's face at his words. Leah grinned back.

'But for now,' Mr Whistler said, settling himself down into his chair and drawing a folder across his desk, 'I think it's best if the four of you stay out of the way. And don't mention this to anyone yet. If Mr Jones finds out that you were the ones who discovered his mistake, well, he might do something rash.'

Leah gulped. She hadn't thought about that.

'Of course, sir,' she said. 'We'll go straight back to Cindy's house.'

'Good,' Mr Whistler said, sounding preoccupied. Then he bowed his head over his work. Taking it as a dismissal, the four children started to leave, but Leah paused when Mr Whistler called after them. He held a sheet of paper out. 'Will one of you give this to Miss Sinclair on your way out, please? Some of her edits have mistakes in them that need to be corrected quickly.'

Leah took the paper, glancing down at the assistant's flowery handwriting, and hurried after her friends.

Outside the office, Miss Sinclair was telling Cindy off with her hands on her hips. But it looked like Cindy didn't care. She was bouncing on the balls of her feet, her eyes bright and her hands clasped in front of her. From her pocket, Leah could hear Marty's squeaks. As she placed the sheet of edits on the PA's desk, Cindy caught her eye and beamed. Leah smiled back. Soon, Mr Jones would be in custody and Nancy would be home.

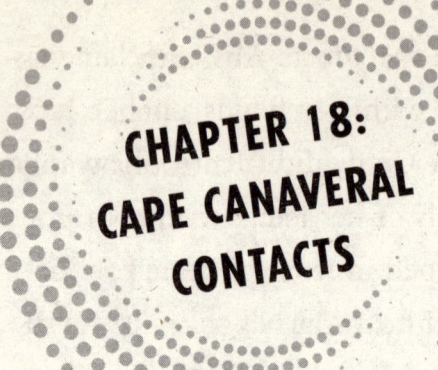

CHAPTER 18: CAPE CANAVERAL CONTACTS

Later that night, Cindy was so excited she could barely sleep.

'Can you believe it?' she burst out more than once, her voice quivering. They'd had dinner with Cindy's gramma earlier and it had been a struggle to stop Cindy from blurting out everything they'd learned, especially when her gramma had looked so sad and stressed about Nancy's disappearance. But now they were all lying beneath their blankets in the privacy of Cindy's bedroom, Cindy's excitement couldn't be contained. 'My mom's coming home tomorrow!'

But there was something bothering Leah. Ever since they'd left the compound earlier that day after speaking to Mr Whistler, her fingers had been straying towards the watch hanging around her neck. They'd left well after noon, so she hadn't expected the watch to send them home immediately, but as the evening had worn on, she'd expected *something* – some kind of sign that they'd completed their mission.

But it never came.

When Cindy's elation finally wore itself out and their new friend dropped into a deep sleep, Leah lay still, hugging the watch to her chest as she waited for midnight to arrive. Next to her, Mimi and George did the same.

But when it turned twelve, the tell-tale tingle of warmth that usually meant they'd completed their mission didn't come. The watch remained still and cold.

Leah let out a disappointed huff. 'Why didn't it work?' she said, turning to her friends. 'Why aren't we home already? What's the watch waiting for?'

George said nothing, his face full of disappointment as he slumped back against his pillows.

Mimi tried to be more positive. 'Hmm,' she said thoughtfully, her fingers twisting in her braids. 'Maybe we can't leave until Nancy is *actually* home. We might have caught her kidnapper, but she's still technically missing, isn't she?'

Leah sighed and rolled onto her back. 'I suppose,' she agreed reluctantly. 'But if that's true, they need to find her fast. The space camp ends tomorrow and Cindy will expect us to go home. We'll be out of time!'

'Don't worry, Leah,' said Mimi. She reached over and patted her arm, yawning. 'I bet we'll be home by tomorrow night.'

But even with her friend's reassurances, Leah couldn't shake the feeling that something wasn't right. It all felt too easy. She drifted in and out of sleep all night, tossing and turning, whilst images of exploding rockets plagued her dreams. She didn't let go of the watch once.

The next morning, Leah's eyes felt gritty, as if sand were lodged beneath her lids, and a dull ache pounded behind her ears. She hadn't been able to sleep properly, her mind filled with the sense that something wasn't quite right. Besides, after all the running around yesterday, her knee had ached constantly, the pain keeping sleep just out of reach. She was quiet as they made their way to the compound, the bus dropping them at the same spot as the day before.

Out of habit, the four of them drifted towards the West Computing Area. Cindy was a ball of barely restrained energy, buzzing with the possibility that her mother was coming home. What with the events of the past twenty-four hours, she hadn't mentioned the space camp, and she didn't now either. Leah was relieved. She supposed that Cindy was too distracted to care about what Leah's fictional teacher might have to say about their absence.

The human computers were hard at work when the children arrived. Some of them lifted their heads as Leah and her friends settled themselves at Nancy's desk, pitying smiles on their faces. Abruptly, Leah realized that none of them would know yet that Nancy's kidnapper had been found and that she would be back soon. After all, Mr Whistler had asked them not to say anything.

'Gee, we made a bit of a mess of my mom's desk yesterday,' Cindy said, fiddling with her hair ribbons. The desk's surface was littered with Nancy's papers, the neat piles had been knocked over in the children's haste to find her notes to show Mr Whistler. The evidence they'd found was folded and tucked in Cindy's pocket, with Marty guarding it closely. Leah had thought it was a bit strange that Mr Whistler hadn't wanted to hold on to the pages of incorrect sums to show the police, but she supposed he thought he wouldn't need them.

'Eesh, you're right,' George said, biting his lip and running a hand through his curls. 'Let's try to tidy up a bit so it's all ready for when she comes back.'

They set about gathering up the papers and folders. Leah grabbed a few sheets, shuffling them into some kind of order. As she did, a small scrap fell out and fluttered to the floor. She crouched down to grab it, but when she saw what was written on it, she paused, a slight frown on her face.

'What's up, L?' Mimi said, noticing that she'd gone quiet.

'Nothing, it's just . . .' Leah straightened up, holding the paper out for the others to see. 'Look.'

George tilted his head to one side. 'What is it? A phone number?'

'Yeah, but look at the name printed above it,' Leah said.

'Sam?' Cindy frowned.

'Hey!' Mimi exclaimed. 'Wasn't Mr Jones on the phone to someone called Sam?'

Leah nodded. 'And Mr Whistler, when we went into his office.'

'So?' Cindy asked.

'Well, don't you think that's weird? They were both talking to the same person.' Leah paused, thinking. 'And neither of them seemed very happy with him.'

'Mr Jones told him to get the new rocket ready,' Mimi said. She wrinkled her nose as she considered this, and then asked Cindy, 'Where did the first Intrepid rocket launch from?'

'Cape Canaveral, of course,' Cindy replied. 'In Florida. It's where most of the big launches happen.'

'Why does your mum have the number of someone working there?' Leah asked.

'I . . .' Cindy paused, and then she shook her head. 'I don't know actually. Usually, she doesn't have anything to do with the ground team in Florida. She just does the math.'

'Maybe we should ring the number,' Mimi suggested. 'This Sam might have information about where Nancy is.'

'Good idea, Meems,' Leah said with a firm nod. She looked around the busy computing room. 'Cindy, is there somewhere we can call him without being overheard?'

But Cindy was shaking her head. She looked faintly annoyed. 'Hang on,' she said. 'We don't *need* to ring Sam. We've already caught Mr Jones, and my mom's going to come back any time now! What more do we need to know?'

Leah looked at Mimi and George. Her fingers

twitched, but she resisted the urge to reach for the watch. Cindy didn't know anything about where they'd really come from. How could she explain that she had a feeling there were still some loose ends, even with Mr Jones in police custody?

In the end, it was George who answered. He gave a casual shrug. 'Look, it can't hurt, can it? Besides, Sam might be able to give us even more evidence to use against Mr Jones. The more dirt we have on him, the better, right?'

Cindy was silent, but then she sighed. 'I guess so. And at least it'll help fill the time until my mom gets here. There isn't a phone we can use round here without being overheard, though. We should head over to the Aeronautics building. There are tons in the offices there.'

Clutching Sam's number in her hand, Leah and her friends made the trip over to Mr Whistler's building. They walked quickly. Leah felt like she ought to run, but her knee gave her a warning twinge when she tried.

She didn't know why, but she felt Sam would have the answers they needed.

They waved hello to Apollo as they bounded up the steps. The old dog wagged his tail at the sight of them, and Leah guessed that the fact he didn't bark at them meant he now considered them friends. Inside, they easily found an empty office with a phone.

'Who's going to call?' George asked as they stood clustered around the empty desk.

'Me, of course,' Mimi said imperiously. 'Cindy, will you dial the number?'

Leah handed Cindy the paper and watched as her friend spun the dial, hooking her fingers in the holes and twisting. When she was done, there was a pause and the familiar *beep beep beep* of the ringing tone.

It didn't take long. A man answered, and if Leah and her friends leaned forward, they could just hear his replies.

'Hello, this is Sam Chapman.' His voice was deep and raspy. In the background, Leah could hear loud banging.

'Oh, yes, hello, my name's Amelia and I work with Mrs Nancy Grant,' Mimi said.

There was a pause, and then Sam said, 'What can I do for you, Miss Amelia?' He sounded wary, as if he were considering all of his words carefully.

'Well, I'm calling on behalf of Mrs Grant. She just—'

But Sam cut Mimi off before she could say anything about the kidnapping. 'Look, I don't have anything more to say to her. I told her everything I knew on Wednesday.'

Leah's eyes widened as she stared at Cindy, Mimi and George. Wednesday was the night that Nancy went missing!

Mimi's voice was smooth as she replied. 'Yes, I'm aware of that. It's just that Mrs Grant is worried that she's forgotten something. Could you just repeat what you discussed and I'll make a note?'

Leah bit her lip.

But it appeared that Sam was too busy thinking of himself to doubt their story. 'I can't go on the record with any of this,' he said quickly, his words laced with panic. 'They can't know I said anything. I could lose my job!'

'Of course not, of course not,' Mimi assured him. 'I'll leave your name out of it. But if you could just—'

Sam sighed. 'Fine. I'll tell you exactly what I told Mrs Grant. The math for Intrepid One was correct. I checked it myself before the launch. Her numbers were dead on, like they always are.'

'So . . . it wasn't the calculations that made the rocket explode?'

'No. But it's hard to know exactly what *was* responsible.' Sam lowered his voice, but his words became louder, as if he were holding the phone closer to his mouth. 'Things have become . . . difficult here at Cape Canaveral. I'm losing workers every day to accommodate the budget cuts and, as I told Nancy, although we suspect the fault with the navigation system was responsible for the explosion, I don't have concrete proof, nor the time or people to investigate it properly. And now we've got the second launch today. I'm telling you, it's a bad idea. Intrepid Two has the exact same navigation system as the rocket that exploded. If the first system was installed incorrectly, this one will be too.'

'Does Mr Whistler know about this?' Mimi demanded.

'Of course!' Sam laughed. 'But he's convinced it was a one-off problem. It's like he's determined to ignore all the evidence I've shown him, and I just have to do what I'm told, don't I? I know the President is breathing down his neck about this and we've only got one shot to impress him, but...' Sam paused as someone in the background called his name. 'Look, are we done here? I've got a rocket to get ready.'

'Yes, thank you, Mr Chapman,' Mimi said. 'You've been most helpful.' The line went dead and Mimi replaced the receiver with a click.

There was a beat of silence as the children all looked at each other, trying to digest what Sam had told them.

'It was never the math,' Cindy said finally, her brow creased in confusion. 'Mom's numbers were always right.'

'But what about the mismatched numbers

on your mum's and Mr Jones's notes?' George asked. 'Can I see them again? Maybe we missed something.'

'I don't know,' Cindy said, shrugging and handing the folded papers over. 'But I don't think you're going to find anything new in there, George. Sam said the sums weren't the problem.'

'What about that technical fault? Why has no one mentioned that before? When we've overheard people talking about the crash, all they keep focusing on is the calculations!' Mimi wrinkled her nose.

'Maybe no one is talking about it because no one knows,' Leah said slowly. 'It sounds like your mum stumbled on something she wasn't supposed to, Cindy.' The puzzle pieces were rearranging themselves in Leah's brain, slotting together in new ways. But she still felt like something was missing.

'Hey,' George said with a thoughtful frown. 'When Mr Whistler was on the phone yesterday, wasn't he talking about budget cuts? And the President?'

Leah nodded. 'And Sam said he knew about the technical fault. You don't think . . . ?'

Cindy held up her hand, swallowing hard. 'Hang on. Are you saying you think Mr Whistler is mixed up with my mom's disappearance? Because that's just ridiculous. Mr Whistler has known my mom for years. He's the reason she got her job in the first place. Besides, we checked the punch-in log. He wasn't even in the building when she went missing.' Cindy's voice was getting angrier and angrier.

Leah took a deep breath. She hadn't meant to offend Cindy and she opened her mouth to apologize, but the words lodged themselves in her throat as she saw a familiar figure stride past the office door.

It was Mr Jones.

He was walking with a bounce in his step, his glasses perched high on his nose. In one hand he held a steaming cup of coffee, and in the other he had a folder.

'Hey,' Leah said. 'I thought Mr Whistler was having him arrested!'

The others turned, catching sight of Mr Jones as he disappeared around a corner. Cindy's anger dissolved into confusion. 'I don't understand,' she mumbled. 'Why isn't he with the police?'

'Children!'

Leah jumped as a familiar figure filled the doorway. It was Mr Whistler. He was smiling at them, his perfect, white teeth gleaming.

Leah immediately shuffled closer to her friends, hiding the phone behind them. She could see that Sam's number was clenched in Cindy's palm. There was no way that Mr Whistler knew what they'd been doing, was there? Leah swallowed nervously as she wondered how much he'd overheard.

'Good morning, sir,' Cindy said with a polite dip of her chin.

'I've been looking for you, Cindy,' Mr Whistler said. 'Your grandmother called. She's coming to collect you on the bus and wants you to wait for her in your mother's building.'

Cindy's lips jutted out in a pout. 'Why?' she demanded, and then, as if remembering who she was talking to, she added, 'Sir.'

Mr Whistler clasped his hands in front of him. 'She feels that maybe you should be at home together whilst we wait on news about your mom. You can come back once the investigation is finished.'

Leah looked at Cindy. Was it possible that Mr Whistler didn't know Mr Jones hadn't been arrested yet?

'No problem, sir,' Cindy said, starting towards the door. 'We'll head right over.' Leah, Mimi and George started to follow her, but Mr Whistler held up his hand, stopping them.

'Shouldn't you three be heading back to the space camp?' he said, raising his eyebrow. 'I've noticed you've not been spending much time over there. Should I call your teacher?'

Leah glanced at her friends, trying not to let her panic show in her eyes. 'Uh . . .' Mr Whistler had backed them into a corner. If they said no, he'd ring the space camp for sure. 'Yes, sir, you're right. We'll go back straight away.'

Cindy shot them a pained look. 'I'll speak to

you later, okay?' she said before leaving the office.

Mr Whistler gave them a patient smile. 'I'll call the space camp later to check on you three.' And then he too left, heading in the opposite direction to Cindy.

Alone in the office with George and Mimi, Leah ground her teeth in frustration. Her belly writhed like a tangle of snakes. She didn't know what, but *something* wasn't right.

'I hate it when she gets that look on her face,' George said quietly. He and Mimi were staring at Leah.

'What look?' Leah demanded.

'The look that says you're going to do something potentially dangerous,' Mimi said matter-of-factly.

'I think we should follow Mr Whistler,' Leah said. She peered out of the office and stared after Mr Whistler's retreating back.

'Why?' George asked, exasperated.

'Because I think he knows more than he's letting on,' Leah replied, and then, before George or Mimi could protest, she rushed out into the corridor after him, ignoring the painful twinge in her knee.

Behind her, she could hear her friends hissing her name, but she didn't stop. It was like there was a hook in her chest that was towing her after the director of the NACA. He was up to something.

George and Mimi quickly caught up with her. George was muttering anxiously under his breath, but Leah ignored him. She kept a healthy distance between them and Mr Whistler, ducking into the shadows along the edge of the corridor if it seemed as if he was going to look over his shoulder. But he never did.

They followed him through a set of double doors and then down a short flight of stairs. They left the white-painted walls behind them, trading them for rough, plastered ones the colour of hot chocolate. Up ahead, Mr Whistler turned left and Leah hurried to follow him. But when she turned the corner, he was nowhere to be seen.

Instead, ahead of her was an open doorway.

Leah, Mimi and George crept towards it, trying not to make any sound. Leah poked her head through the door frame. There was no one inside and she couldn't see Mr Whistler anywhere. Cautiously, they stepped inside.

The room looked like a windowless basement. It was filled with big cardboard boxes, and along one wall was a table holding various tools and lengths of rope.

'Where did he go?' Mimi whispered, looking left and right. 'He must be here somewhere.'

'Of course I am,' came Mr Whistler's voice. Leah spun around with a gasp to find the director of the NACA standing behind them. 'After all, I was hoping you'd follow me.'

And then his expression shifted. In an instant, the kind man they'd grown to know over the last couple of days drained away like water down a plughole. In his place was someone much harder and crueller, his face full of menace as he glared at them.

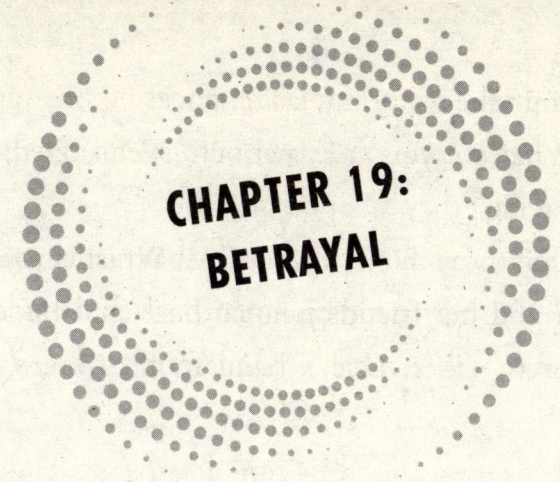

CHAPTER 19: BETRAYAL

'Mr Whistler?' George asked, his voice hitching uncertainly. 'What's going on?'

Mr Whistler's face became even darker as he glowered at them, as if a thundercloud had passed overhead and cast his features in a stormy shadow. 'I think you know exactly what's going on. That's the problem, isn't it?'

'Sir . . .' Leah began. Her hands felt hot and itchy. She clamped them together to stop her fingers from trembling with fear.

Mr Whistler talked over her as if she hadn't spoken. 'You just couldn't help yourselves, could you? Had to keep poking your noses into business that didn't concern you. Well, I won't let you ruin everything I've worked for. I won't let you take away my last chance!'

'What are you *talking* about?' Mimi cried, her eyes wide.

'Don't play dumb with me!' Mr Whistler roared. Leah and her friends jumped back and huddled closer together. Leah's hand found Mimi's and

squeezed. Mr Whistler's face was a mask of fury as he loomed over them, his lips pulled back from his teeth like a wild animal's. 'I was happy to let you continue your little detective charade. After all, you were *helping* me. Heck, I couldn't believe it when you came to me with your suspicions about Mr Jones.' He snorted. 'As if *he* has the brains or the guts to come up with something like this.'

Leah looked at her friends as Mr Whistler spoke. Did he mean that Mr Jones had nothing to do with Nancy's disappearance?

'No,' Mr Whistler said, shaking his head. He was breathing hard, and he paused as he tried to regain control, his expression smoothing out. 'There was only one other person I could trust to help me, and it certainly *wasn't* Mr Jones.'

'H-help you do what, sir?' George stammered. He was still clutching the papers that Cindy had given to him, and the edges trembled as his fingers shook.

Mr Whistler chuckled. It was a dry, raspy noise. 'Still trying to protect yourselves, huh?' He spread his hands wide, palms facing upwards.

'Look, I know you all know. I heard you on the phone with Sam. Now, if it were just little Cindy, I'd be able to deal with her, but you three are a trickier problem to tackle. You just won't let it go, will you? And now you know too much. Just like *she* did.'

'Like who did?' Mimi whispered.

Mr Whistler was silent as he stared at them, cocking one eyebrow. It was almost as if he were waiting for them to piece it together.

'Just like Nancy,' Leah said slowly, the realization chilling her like a bucket of ice.

Mr Whistler frowned. 'Nancy was a problem, so I dealt with her.'

'What did you do?' Leah growled. Her muscles were bunched up tight, and the only things stopping her from leaping at the NACA director were her own fear and her friend's hand clamped tightly around her own. 'She figured it out, didn't she?' Leah whispered, her mind racing. 'She knew that her calculations weren't the reason Intrepid One exploded. It was the technical fault with the navigation system. The one that *you* knew about but didn't do anything about because . . .' Leah racked her brains, trying to remember everything she'd heard over the last few days. And then it clicked. 'Because of the budget cuts! You needed to save money, so there weren't enough staff to make sure everything was safe. Besides, if the President found out there was something wrong with the way Intrepid One had been built, he might have called the whole thing off. So you just pretended nothing was wrong and you went ahead with the launch.' Leah's eyes widened. 'It was *your* fault that rocket exploded!'

Mr Whistler's mouth twisted into a sneer. 'So clever, aren't you?'

Leah's entire body was vibrating with anger. She was scared, but it was nothing compared to her fury and frustration. She thought about poor Nancy and Cindy. They'd both trusted this man, but he was a liar.

'Where did you take Nancy?' Leah snapped.

But Mr Whistler gave an ugly laugh, shaking his head. 'This isn't a film, you stupid child. I'm not going to stand here and make my confession to you, unveiling all of my plans. And even if I wanted to do that, I don't have time. Today is a big day. My chance to prove myself once and for all.'

Leah's mind raced. 'Intrepid Two. You're still going to launch the rocket.'

'That's right.' Mr Whistler smirked. He turned towards the door, but Mimi's shout stopped him.

'You can't! The navigation system—'

Mr Whistler spoke over her, his voice cracking like a whip. 'This won't be like last time! That was a one-time error. Intrepid Two is a completely different rocket, and in an hour and a half the President won't have any reason to doubt me. The world will witness the first *manned* space flight and the United States of America *will* beat the Soviet Union!'

'What do you mean?' Leah didn't know why, but the way Mr Whistler said the word 'manned' made her heart stutter. It was like he was telling a joke, but she couldn't understand why it was funny.

Mr Whistler gripped the door handle, stepping

out into the corridor. 'It's nothing for you to worry about,' he assured her. 'After all, you'll be stuck in here . . . until I can come back and deal with you when this is all over.' He smiled at them, his white teeth reminding Leah of a shark's.

And then he slammed the door shut. There was a rattle, a thunk, and then a decisive click.

He'd locked them in.

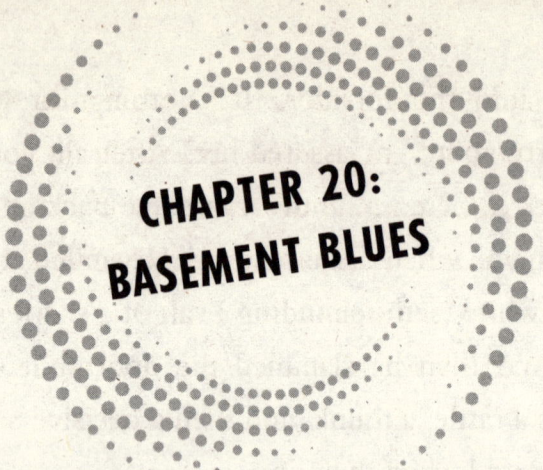

CHAPTER 20: BASEMENT BLUES

Wrenching herself away from her friends, Leah flew towards the door. She grasped the handle, rattling it desperately. But it was no use.

They were trapped.

Leah beat her fists against the wood. 'Help!' she cried. 'Help! We're stuck!'

'L, no one is going to hear you down here!' Mimi said, rushing to her side. Her hands were trembling, but Leah could see she was trying to stay calm. The same couldn't be said of George. He was pacing, one hand fisted in his hair whilst the other clutched Nancy's notes. He was muttering to himself, his voice too low for Leah and Mimi to hear.

'Someone might.' Leah broke off. She

hammered the door harder, but it didn't do anything, except make the side of her fists ache.

'Stop!' George said, coming to a halt and spinning to face his friends with wide eyes. 'This obviously isn't how we're going to get out!'

'Well, what do you suggest then?' Leah demanded, whirling towards him. 'I'm not just going to stand here and do nothing.'

'Don't have a go at me,' George snapped. '*You're* the one who wanted to follow Mr Whistler in the first place.'

'Oh, so this is my fault?' Leah exclaimed.

'If you'd just been patient and *waited* for us, we would have told you—'

Leah cut George off, her frustration bubbling up to boiling point. 'Right. Because you two know so much more than I do, don't you?'

'Oh, will you both give it a rest?' Mimi bellowed. Her voice was so loud it made both Leah and George jump. She had her hands twisted into her braids, as if holding onto her head would stop it from exploding. She took a deep breath. 'Arguing with each other won't get us anywhere.'

All of a sudden, the emotion drained from Leah's body. She and George looked at each other sheepishly. Leah's cheeks burned. She'd let her emotions take over, but she shouldn't take it out on her friends.

'Sorry, George,' she mumbled. 'I didn't mean . . .'

'No, it's fine, I'm sorry too,' George replied.

Leah gave him a small smile.

'Right, now that we've sorted that out,' Mimi said, exasperated. 'We need a plan. Are there any other ways we can get out of here?'

'There aren't any windows,' George pointed out helpfully. 'Maybe we can break the door handle?'

Leah shook her head. 'Breaking the handle won't break the lock.' She sighed. 'If only I really *was* a master lock-picker like Cindy thought I was.'

'Leah! That's it!' Mimi cried. 'You're a genius!'

'I . . . I am?' Leah raised her eyebrows in confusion.

'We can open this lock the same way we opened Mr Jones's door!' Mimi babbled, her face lit with excitement.

Leah realized it at the same time George did. They looked at each other, grinning. 'The key!'

'I have it in here,' George said, threading his hand through his hoody pocket. He frowned. 'Or at least, I thought I did . . .'

'What do you mean?' Leah asked.

'Well, it was here this morning, but . . .' George patted down his jeans too, but his expression was full of horror as he looked up at his friends. 'It's gone!'

'No, it can't be,' Mimi said firmly, shaking her head. 'Maybe you gave it to me?' But when she dug her fingers into her pockets, the only thing she found was the compass.

Leah knew that George hadn't given her the key, but she checked anyway, just in case. Automatically, she reached for the watch hanging around her neck and swallowed her sigh of relief when her fingers found the familiar metal chain sitting against her skin. Next, she slid her hand into one of her shorts pockets, where she kept the magnifying glass.

She gasped.

'The magnifying glass is gone too!' she cried.

Suddenly, being locked in the basement wasn't the worst thing that happened to them that day.

'Oh no, oh no, oh no,' George moaned. 'This is *so* bad.'

'But where could they have gone?' Mimi said. Leah could tell she was trying to stay calm, but her lips were pressed together in a thin line.

Leah thought back to this morning. She was sure the magnifying glass had been in her pocket at breakfast. But then they'd got on the bus and sat in the West Computing Area before moving over to the Aeronautics building.

'They could have fallen out anywhere,' Leah said grimly.

Without the key, their hopes of escaping the basement dwindled to zero. Desperate, Mimi looked through some of the boxes to see if there was *anything* they could use to force the lock, but all she found were piles of plastic tubing and lumps of metal.

'Rocket stuff,' she groaned as she sank into

a heap in front of the table. Leah and George joined her.

'What are we going to do?' George whispered. 'Nancy is still in danger, and if we don't rescue her, we won't be able to go home. We'll . . . we'll be stuck here forever.' His voice wobbled and his eyes were bright.

Usually, Leah had some kind of plan. There was always something they could try or some way they could escape, but now . . . now she was out of ideas. She leaned her head against George's shoulder, feeling hopelessness settle over her in a numb blanket. She thought that maybe she should cry, but her eyes were dry, as if her body couldn't summon even one more ounce of feeling. She didn't even have the energy to tell George it was going to be okay. She didn't want to lie to him.

'We'll just have to wait,' she said, holding his hand. 'Someone will find us eventually.'

'Or Mr Whistler will come back,' George replied, his voice thick with tears.

Leah squeezed her eyes shut. She didn't want

to think about what would happen when Mr Whistler decided to return. What would he do to them?

'I knew there was something fishy about him,' Mimi suddenly said.

Leah snorted. 'You did not.'

Mimi was silent, and then she sighed. 'Okay, I didn't. He seemed so nice!'

'We jumped to conclusions.' George sniffed. 'Again.'

'I really thought he was on Nancy and Cindy's side. I thought he was on *our* side.' Mimi sounded disappointed.

Leah had thought the same. Cindy had said that Mr Whistler had been friends with her family for years.

'I want to know how he did it,' Mimi said, frowning. 'The kidnapping, I mean. Mr Whistler left way before Nancy disappeared. The security guard himself said that he saw him get in his car and drive off.'

'Argh!' George shouted, his voice quivering with anger. He was still clutching Nancy's notes, and now he threw the papers into the air. 'This is useless! We're going round in circles and it's not getting us any closer to finding Nancy and going home.' The tears he'd been trying to hold back now suddenly flooded down his cheeks.

'Oh, George,' Leah said, feeling her own throat growing thick. She put her arm around George's shoulder and hugged him tight. On his other side, Mimi did the same. 'Don't cry.'

'I'm never touching that watch again,' George sobbed. 'I'm officially retired from time travel.'

Leah choked on a laugh. If only it were that easy.

But seeing George get so upset seemed to break the spell weighing Leah down. What were they doing, all huddled on the floor like this? Maybe everything *was* hopeless, but they had to at least *try* to get out. They had to *try* to get home.

'Come on,' Leah said, when George's tears had stopped. He wiped his eyes. 'When have we ever given up? We're the Wonder Team. We're going to get out of this place.' She jumped up, holding her hands out to Mimi and George. They took them, and Leah hauled her friends to their feet.

'Leah, we've tried everything . . .' Mimi said, but Leah was shaking her head. She began picking up the papers that George had thrown on the floor.

'What about that rope?' she said as she picked up the last sheet. 'We can—' She broke off abruptly.

'We can what?' George said.

But Leah wasn't listening. She was staring at the locked door. Had she heard a noise coming from outside?

'What's the matter?' Mimi asked, frowning.

Leah shook her head. 'I thought I heard . . .' She trailed off.

Suddenly, the door handle rattled.

They froze. Was it Mr Whistler? Had he come back for them? What if he'd decided to get rid of them once and for all?

Leah thought she might be sick. She swallowed thickly.

The handle turned and the door swung open.

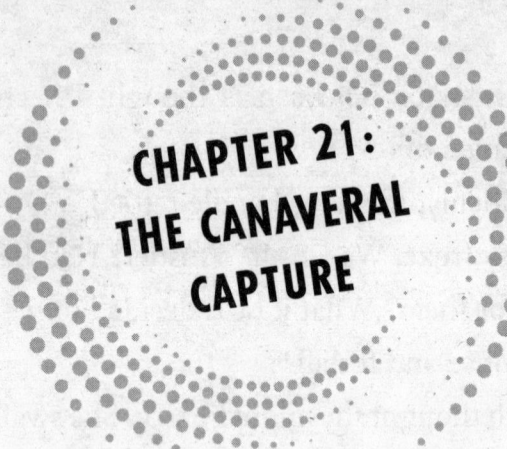

CHAPTER 21: THE CANAVERAL CAPTURE

Leah gasped as the door crashed against the wall with a ferocious bang. She braced herself for the sight of Mr Whistler, his silhouette looming, ready to lead her and her friends to their doom.

But it wasn't Mr Whistler.

It was Cindy!

The white ribbons in her hair almost seemed to glow in the darkness of the corridor. She stared at them, her eyes wide and her mouth hanging slightly open. In one hand she was gripping the magnifying glass, and in the other was the key.

'Cindy!' Mimi cried, her voice so full of relief, Leah thought she might start to cry. And then they were all rushing towards each other, crashing together in a tangle of limbs as they hugged.

'What are you guys *doing* down here?' Cindy demanded.

Leah waved a paper-filled hand. 'We'll tell you in a sec, but first, how did you find us? How did you get *those*?' She pointed to the two magical items that Cindy was gripping.

Cindy stared at the magnifying glass and the key. 'It was the strangest thing,' she told them. 'I was walking back to the West Computing Area when my dress pockets suddenly got really heavy.' She stuck her hands into the two pockets on either side of her dress. 'And then when I stopped to check, they were just in there. Like magic!'

'Like magic,' Leah repeated. She smiled at Mimi and George.

'I took them out, and they were really hot in my hand. And they were pulsing, like they wanted me to do something with them. I got this really bad stomach ache, and I just knew that if I didn't move, something horrible was going to happen.' Cindy shuddered at the memory. 'So then I looked through the magnifying glass and followed the sparkly dust all the way here and the key opened the door.'

'I promise I'll never say a bad thing about that magnifying glass again,' George vowed, pressing a hand to his heart. Mimi laughed.

'But how did you get in here?' Cindy asked, frowning in confusion. 'And why was the door locked?'

Leah and her friends exchanged a glance. She took a deep breath and started at the beginning, telling Cindy how they'd followed Mr Whistler after she'd left and how he'd locked them in the basement so he could launch Intrepid Two.

'And then we figured out that he'd been cutting corners and ignoring safety regulations, but that's not the worst part. The worst part is that he confessed to kidnapping your mum. He wouldn't tell us what he'd done with her, though,' Leah finished, spreading her hands wide. 'We were just trying to find a way out of here so we could tell someone when you showed up.'

Cindy's eyes were wide as she stared at Leah. 'Mr Whistler? No! I already told you. He wouldn't—'

'Cindy!' Mimi interrupted, not unkindly. 'He *confessed* to us! He told us he did it!'

Cindy's mouth gaped and she shook her head. 'But . . . but . . .' Her gaze flicked frantically between the three of them, and then, as the truth finally hit her, her face crumpled. 'He did this? He took my mom?' Her voice cracked.

'I'm so sorry,' Leah said quietly.

'I just don't understand! He's always supported Mom and the rest of the computers. Why would he do something like this?' Cindy looked at them pleadingly.

'It wasn't just him, either,' George added.

'You mean there are more people involved?' Cindy looked horrified.

Mimi nodded. 'That's right. Before he locked us in here, he told us he was working with someone. Someone he trusted.'

'Who?' Cindy demanded.

'Well, we haven't quite figured that out yet,' Leah replied with a wince.

'I bet it's Mr Jones!' Cindy cried, curling her hands into fists. From her pocket, Marty let out an indignant *squeak*.

But George was already shaking his head. 'No, no, it's definitely *not* Mr Jones. Mr Whistler told us that he'd never work with him.'

Leah listened to her friends as they fired their theories back and forth. She wanted to know who Mr Whistler was working with, too, but they were up against a ticking clock. Mr Whistler had said Intrepid Two was going to launch in an hour and a half, and Leah kept thinking of the way he'd looked when he'd left the basement. He'd been wearing an expression of complete satisfaction, as though everything was going just as he had hoped. As Leah stooped to pick up the rest of Nancy's notes littering the floor, she had a terrible feeling in her stomach that his plans weren't finished yet and that there was something even worse to come.

'We need to get out of here and get up to the launch room,' she said suddenly, interrupting her friends. 'We might not know who Mr Whistler is working with, but, thanks to Sam, we know that Intrepid Two isn't safe. It's got a faulty navigation system, just like Intrepid One.'

'We've got to stop that launch before it's too late,' Cindy gasped.

Leah nodded. 'But time's running out. We've got less than an hour and a half. When Mr Whistler left us here, he said . . .'

Leah suddenly tailed off, going rigid as Mr Whistler's last words played in her mind. What was it he'd said?

The world will witness the first manned *space flight and the United States of America* will *beat the Soviet Union!*

Leah sucked in a lungful of air. Suddenly, the room felt too small, her sweatshirt too tight around her neck. The notes crinkled in her hands as her fingers tightened. In her mind, she saw a map with a red circle inked upon it.

'Oh no!' she breathed, dismay contorting her features.

'What is it, L?' Mimi asked. Behind her, George and Cindy were staring at her with concern.

'I . . . I know where Nancy is,' Leah replied. The others looked at each other in excitement, but Leah felt like the world was spinning. Everything swirled and swam like some horrible dream.

'Where?' Cindy was demanding, her expression fierce.

Leah swallowed. Her tongue felt thick as she forced herself to say the next words. 'She's in Florida. At Cape Canaveral. Inside Intrepid Two.'

CHAPTER 22: THE MISS SINCLAIR AFFAIR

Leah's words hung in the air.

'What?' Mimi choked out.

Leah shook her head. 'Mr Whistler said the world was about to witness the first "manned" space flight. But I haven't heard anyone mention any astronauts. Have you?'

'Putting Nancy in that rocket . . . She'll die!' Mimi said in dismay.

'I think that might be the point,' Leah said quietly. 'Remember when Nancy told us that the rockets aren't built to return to Earth in one piece? Well, this must be Mr Whistler's way of stopping her from telling everyone what she knows.'

Cindy had been frozen in silence since Leah's revelation, but now she turned and sprinted out of the basement.

'Cindy!' Leah shouted after her. She turned to Mimi and George. 'Come on, we've got to stop her. She can't just go barging into the launch room without any proper evidence!'

Leah, Mimi and George raced out of the basement, taking the stairs two at a time. They could see Cindy ahead, her dress swishing around her calves. Leah tried to speed up to catch her, but then a bolt of pain shot up her leg.

'Argh!' she cried, stumbling into the wall. She clutched her knee, her teeth gritted as the pain slowly faded. It still throbbed a little, though, as if it were irritated that Leah had even tried to run.

'L!' Mimi panted. 'Are you okay?'

'I'm fine, I'm fine!' Leah said tightly. 'Just stop Cindy! I'll catch up.'

For a moment Mimi looked like she might refuse, but then she nodded and sprinted off, George trailing after her.

Leah waited until the pain was manageable and then she hobbled after them.

It didn't take her long to find them. Mimi had

cornered Cindy in an empty office – and they were arguing.

'I need to save my mom!' Cindy spat.

'I know.' Mimi nodded, clearly trying to stay calm. 'But if you're going, we're all going together and we need to have a plan.'

'We don't have much time! There must be less than an hour left until—' Cindy began, but Leah interrupted her.

'You're right, time *is* running out,' she said. 'But there's no point rushing in without a plan. We have to work out what we're going to say.'

Cindy looked like she was only seconds away from bursting into tears.

'Look, I know you're scared,' Leah said. She couldn't even imagine how she'd be acting if it was her mum inside that rocket. The thought alone was enough to make her shudder. 'But we're going to save your mum. Do you trust me?'

Cindy stared at her. Finally, she nodded. 'Yes,' she whispered, dropping her eyes and hanging her head.

'Okay,' Leah said. Her whole body felt as if tiny

lightning bolts were zapping through it. They *were* going to save Nancy, but first they needed to work out how they were going to convince everyone they were telling the truth.

'We'll need concrete proof that your mum's inside that rocket,' George said. 'Like a picture or something.'

'Well, how are we supposed to get that?' Cindy protested. 'Florida is *miles* away from here!'

Leah bit her lip. Cindy was right. They couldn't just drive up to the launch pad and take a photo. They didn't even *know* anyone who lived in Florida . . .

Wait . . . yes, they did!

'We'll call Sam!' Leah cried triumphantly.

Cindy's eyebrows shot up. 'Sam?'

Leah nodded enthusiastically. 'Yeah! Mimi, you still have his phone number, don't you? If we ring him, he can—'

'Cindy?' a familiar voice interrupted.

The four children turned to see Miss Sinclair standing in the doorway.

'Miss Sinclair!' Cindy gasped, and she ran

towards the PA, wrapping her arms around her waist and hugging her hard.

'Oh!' Miss Sinclair exclaimed. 'What's wrong, honey?'

Before Leah could stop her, words began tumbling out of Cindy's mouth. 'It's Mr Whistler! He's the one who kidnapped my mom, and now she's locked inside Intrepid Two and he's going to launch the rocket with her trapped inside!'

Miss Sinclair's eyes were wide. 'Cindy! What a terrible thing to say!'

'It's true, I promise!' Cindy insisted.

Miss Sinclair opened her mouth to reply, but Leah got there first. 'She's right,' she said. 'Mr Whistler confessed everything.'

'After he locked us inside the basement!' Mimi added with a scowl.

Miss Sinclair stared at them, her mouth open as she digested everything they'd told her. Leah was surprised to feel a surge of relief as a weight seemed to slip from her shoulders. For once, it was nice to tell a grown-up and know they would be able to help.

But then Miss Sinclair's eyes flashed to the papers that Leah was holding in her hand.

'What have you got there?' she asked. She disentangled herself from Cindy's hug and took a step into the office.

Leah frowned in confusion. 'These? They're Nancy's and Mr Jones's notes from Intrepid One.'

Miss Sinclair's eyebrows lifted. 'And why have you got them?'

'We were looking for clues!' Cindy explained eagerly, rushing to Leah's side. 'We noticed that Mr Jones's notes didn't match Mom's exactly, so we wanted to compare. But that's not important. We need to get to the launch room to tell—'

But Miss Sinclair wasn't listening. She cut across Cindy's words. 'Well, I don't think you should be carrying them around. Our work here *is* confidential after all,' she said. She gave a little laugh, but Leah thought her voice sounded strained. 'Why don't I just take them and put them somewhere safe?' She took another step forward.

Leah wasn't sure why, but she took a step back.

Miss Sinclair frowned at the movement. 'Come

on now, Leah,' she said.

It seemed strange to her that, after everything they'd just told Miss Sinclair about Mr Whistler, Intrepid Two and Nancy, the PA was more interested in the notes Leah was holding. Her eyes flicked down to where Nancy's meticulous scrawl filled the pages . . . and she froze.

This was the first time that Leah had looked at the notes properly. Cindy had been the one to examine them after they'd found Mr Jones's calculations, but now it was Leah's eyes that raked over the numbers. Her eyes widened as she noticed that Nancy's handwriting suddenly disappeared midway down the page, replaced by someone

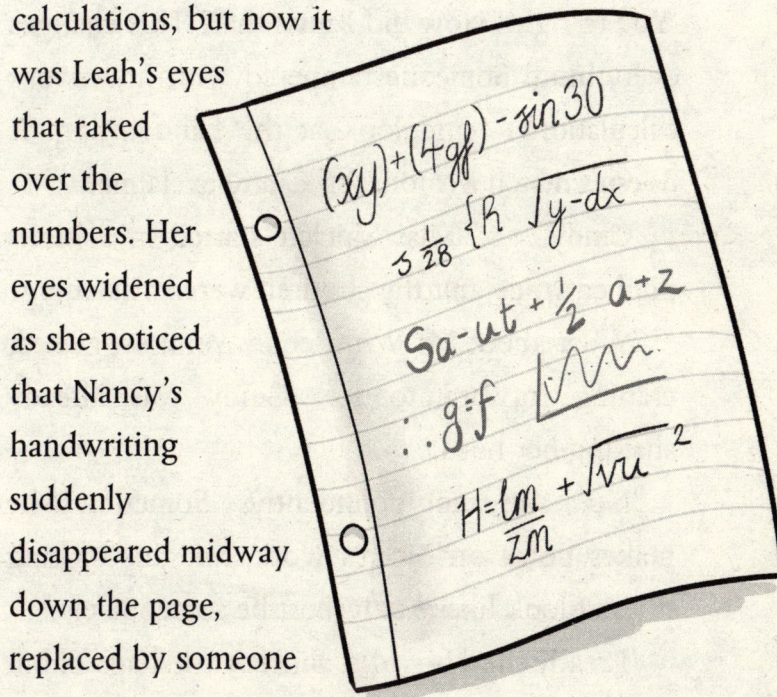

else's. It was only for a few lines, but with the light from the office windows streaming in, the change was obvious.

'These calculations . . .' Leah said slowly, looking up at Miss Sinclair. The PA was watching her with something like fear in her eyes. 'They've been changed.'

'What?' Cindy said abruptly. 'Where? Show me.' Leah handed the notes over, pointing out what she'd seen. Surprise lit Cindy's face. 'You're right! How did I miss that? This changes everything! Someone tampered with my mom's calculations – and look at the handwriting! It doesn't match Mr Jones's!' Cindy exclaimed.

'Cindy . . .' Miss Sinclair started in a high-pitched voice, but the children weren't listening.

'What about Mr Whistler's?' Mimi suggested, craning forward to see. Cindy was already shaking her head.

'No,' she said confidently. 'Sometimes he makes notes on Mom's work, and his writing doesn't look like *that*. It must be someone else.'

'I really think—' Miss Sinclair tried again, but

this time George spoke over her.

'The director of the NACA can't just stroll into the West Computing Area and start tinkering around with important documents. He'd have been seen.'

A terrible suspicion began to bubble in Leah's mind, but before she could say anything, Miss Sinclair jumped in, speaking loudly.

'Don't you think you're racing to conclusions here?' She gave another of her shaky laughs. 'Just because someone's written on your mom's work doesn't mean there's been any foul play. Maybe she was working with someone?'

George shook his head slowly. 'No, Nancy works on her own. She told us that, and she also told us that she's very particular about both her maths *and* her reports.'

'Besides,' Leah said, fixing her gaze on Miss Sinclair's face. 'I know whose handwriting this is.'

'You do?' Cindy cried.

'Really?' Mimi gasped.

Leah nodded. 'I've seen it before, on some

notes that Mr Whistler gave me yesterday. And Miss Sinclair knows whose handwriting it is too.' She looked up at the PA. 'Don't you?'

Miss Sinclair flinched as if Leah had hit her. Her bottom lip wobbled. 'I don't know what you're talking about . . .' she said, but her voice trailed off pathetically.

'I don't understand,' Cindy whispered. 'What's going on?'

Leah turned to her friend. 'Miss Sinclair is the one who tampered with your mum's calculations,' she explained, and Cindy inhaled sharply. 'I'd recognize her writing anywhere. Look at all the flicks and curls on her letters. So it wasn't your mum who wrote the incorrect numbers down. It was Miss Sinclair.'

'You're the one Mr Whistler was talking about,' Mimi said, realization filling her face. 'The only one he could trust to help him.'

'But . . . why would you do that?' Cindy said, turning towards the PA with wide eyes. 'Surely you must have known it would get her into trouble!'

Miss Sinclair opened her mouth to answer, but no words came out. She looked miserable.

'I think that was the point,' Leah said. 'After Intrepid One exploded, Mr Whistler needed *someone* to blame. He chose Nancy.'

Suddenly, Miss Sinclair's face came alive with desperate anger as she stared down at the children. 'We *had* to do it, don't you see?' she cried. 'The launch was a failure and the President was breathing down our necks. He was threatening to shut the programme down! We needed to make a sacrifice!'

'So you chose my mom,' Cindy replied, her face tight with betrayal.

Miss Sinclair winced. 'Oh, Cindy, I didn't want to, but the fact that she was a Black woman meant that no one would question it too much. Mr Whistler said it made her the obvious choice.'

'So when did you decide to kidnap her and lock her inside Intrepid Two then?' George challenged.

'Kidnap her?' Miss Sinclair's face was a mask of shock as she shook her head frantically. 'No, no, you've got it all wrong! I had nothing to do with that!'

'Yeah, right!' Mimi scoffed.

'No, you've got to believe me! I would never set out to *hurt* anyone!' Miss Sinclair said imploringly. 'Especially not Nancy! All I did was change some numbers.'

'But why?' Leah asked. 'Why would you even do that? You must know Nancy would have lost her job.'

Miss Sinclair sighed, her shoulders slumping. 'I did know. And I felt terrible about it!' Her voice hardened. 'But I love my country. Do you have any idea how important this programme is? We *need* to get into space before the Soviets do, and if I can't get up there myself, I'll do everything to make sure that someone else can.'

Mimi frowned. 'What do you mean, if you can't get up there yourself?'

Miss Sinclair thrust her hand into her pocket and drew something small out. She held it out towards them and Leah saw that it was a familiar-looking badge: a small black shield, with a white number eleven in the middle. Dimly, Leah remembered seeing it on Miss Sinclair's desk.

'What's that?' Mimi asked.

'This is the only souvenir I have left from my own days as an astronaut. Or . . . as an *almost* astronaut. They called us the Venus Eleven – eleven women chosen to go into space. We were from different backgrounds, but we were all *brilliant*. We even beat the male astronauts in some tests.' Miss Sinclair sighed wistfully. 'We were going to be the first people to touch the stars.' Then her expression changed, becoming hard and angry. 'But then they took it all away. The government abandoned the project. Told us that only military jet pilots could train as astronauts. Of course, that was the end for us. Women aren't *allowed* to train as military jet pilots. They swept us all off the board, just like that.'

'That . . . doesn't seem fair,' Leah said slowly.

'It wasn't!' Miss Sinclair agreed eagerly. 'We were scrubbed from the history books! But there was nothing we could do. The others . . . after a while, they went on with their lives. I couldn't, though. I came to work here, to do everything I could to make sure that the United States reached space before anyone else did. So when Mr Whistler told me that the President was considering shutting the programme down . . .'

'You did what you had to to save it,' Leah finished, and Miss Sinclair nodded sadly. 'That's why Mr Whistler thought he could trust you. The human computers . . . they said you were fanatical about the space programme, so he knew you'd do whatever it took to keep it alive.'

'But what about my mom?' Cindy suddenly shouted, her face twisted with despair. 'Thanks to you, she's stuck in that rocket!'

Miss Sinclair shook her head frantically. 'I promise, I know nothing about that! Kidnap was never part of the plan.'

'At least, it wasn't,' Leah added grimly, 'until Nancy found out Mr Whistler was cutting corners and launching rockets with faulty navigation systems. Then he couldn't just pin the blame on her. He had to get rid of her entirely.'

'We've got to save her,' Cindy urged. 'We've

wasted so much time! The launch can't be more than forty-five minutes away now!'

'Please, let me help,' Miss Sinclair interjected. She wrung her hands anxiously and her gaze was full of guilt. 'After everything . . . it's the least I can do.'

'There's nothing we want from you,' Cindy snapped, her eyes flashing.

'Actually . . .' Leah said, thinking back to the realization she'd had just before Miss Sinclair had found them. 'There is something you could help us with.'

'Anything!' Miss Sinclair nodded furiously.

Exchanging a look with Mimi and George, Leah said, 'We're going to need access to a telephone.'

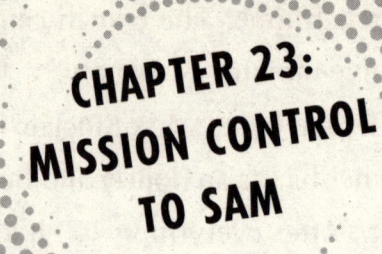

CHAPTER 23: MISSION CONTROL TO SAM

The phone's ringing tone was loud as the four children clustered around an abandoned desk. Mimi once again held the receiver. Despite Cindy's protests and mistrustful glares, they'd followed Miss Sinclair to an empty office near the control room. Leah had hoped the assistant might disappear once they arrived, but she lingered over them, listening, as a click sounded and a familiar voice then said, 'This is Sam Chapman.' His voice was ragged and stressed.

Mimi gripped the phone tightly. 'Hello, this is, uh, Amelia. Nancy's assistant.'

Sam sighed heavily. His voice was muffled, but Leah could just hear him if she crowded closer to the phone. 'Miss Amelia, do you realize what day it is? I do *not* have time—'

'Mr Chapman, this is incredibly important,' Mimi said, her voice hard as iron. 'I know what I'm about to say might sound ridiculous, but I need you to stop the launch of Intrepid Two.'

Sam gave a shocked laugh. 'What? You can't be serious. You're wasting my time!'

'No! Please! I think . . . I think Nancy is trapped inside!' Mimi's voice was full of desperation.

There was a pause, and then Sam laughed again. This time, though, he sounded a little nervous. 'What an awful joke to play, Miss Amelia,' he said. 'As you well know, Intrepid Two isn't built for humans. Anyone inside would almost certainly be killed on the way back down.'

'I know,' Mimi said urgently. 'Which is why you've got to stop the rocket from taking off.'

'Look, I'm a busy man and I don't have time for games,' Sam replied, irritation creeping into his voice. 'I'm hanging up now.'

Mimi began to panic. 'What? No, wait!'

Suddenly, Miss Sinclair lunged forward and snatched the phone from Mimi's grip. 'Mr

Chapman? Hello, it's Miss Sinclair here.'

'*Irene* Sinclair?' Sam sounded surprised.

The assistant's voice was no-nonsense as she said, 'Sam, I really am going to insist that you at least *check* the interior of that rocket. It's probably nothing, but . . . well, I'm here with Nancy's daughter, Cindy, and she's pretty convinced.' She paused, and then added, 'I know Mr Whistler would appreciate it too.'

That seemed to do the trick. Sam huffed out a breath. 'Fine! Hold on a second.' There was a *thunk* and Leah heard Sam call out to someone, 'Pull up the internal rocket feed. Yeah, the central chamber. Yep, okay, here we go.'

There was silence, and then . . .

'HOLY COW!'

His shout echoed down the phone.

'Irene? Cindy? I see her! She's in there. She's really in there!'

Mimi gasped. Leah felt as though the floor were rolling underneath her and, next to her, George looked like he might be sick. Cindy clapped a hand over her mouth, her eyes filling with tears. Miss Sinclair's eyes popped open in shock. Leah realized that, up until that point, the assistant really *hadn't* believed what Leah and her friends had been trying to tell her. Leah knew how she felt. They'd suspected, but now they knew for certain: Nancy was trapped in a rocket due to launch in less than forty minutes.

'How on earth did this happen?' Sam gasped

'You can get her out, can't you?' Cindy shouted, ignoring his question and grabbing the telephone receiver from Miss Sinclair. Tears were falling freely down her cheeks.

There was a long, uncomfortable silence.

'Cindy, I . . .' Sam's voice broke as if he, too, were holding back tears. 'It's too late. There's only forty minutes until the launch. It's not safe for any of my ground crew to get that close!'

'You can't just leave her in there!' Mimi protested.

At the same time, Cindy exclaimed, 'Can't you initiate a launch-pad abort?'

'That's not something we can just *do* by pressing a button,' Sam replied slowly. 'The rocket's internal data systems need to detect a fault before they'll shut down.'

'What are you talking about?' George interrupted. His face was filled with confusion. 'What's a launch-pad abort?'

Cindy turned to him. 'It's a way of stopping the rocket from launching. There are seven seconds between the rocket's orbiter engines engaging and the solid rocket boosters igniting. But if the rocket computers find a problem in that small delay, it'll shut down the whole thing and the rocket will stay on the ground.'

'Cindy, those faults are extremely rare!' Sam interjected. 'And none of them is likely to happen in the next half-hour.'

'Then we'll just make the rocket *think* there's a fault,' Cindy said firmly.

'You're not...' Sam paused, and then, his voice thick with disbelief, said, 'You're not talking about infiltrating the rocket's data systems, are you?'

'I am,' Cindy replied.

'But that's impossible!' Sam protested. 'You'll

only have seven seconds to convince the computer to shut the whole thing down without setting the rocket on fire. Even my best engineers couldn't manage that!'

'Well, I'm not one of your best engineers,' Cindy snapped. 'I'm better.'

And then, before Leah or her friends could stop her, Cindy slammed the phone down, cutting Sam off.

'What are you doing?' Mimi cried. 'We needed him to call the control room to tell them about your mum!'

Cindy shook her head. 'What's the use of him telling them if he's not going to do anything to get her out?' she challenged, her expression fierce. 'No, we're going to have to do this ourselves.'

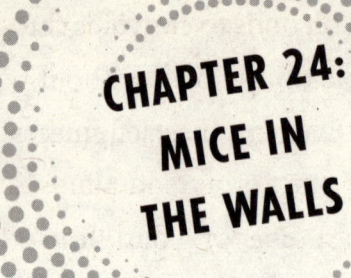

CHAPTER 24: MICE IN THE WALLS

'Are you sure this is a good idea?' George panted, trying his best to keep up with Cindy as she marched down the corridor towards the control room.

'I have to admit, I'm with George,' Miss Sinclair said, struggling to match Cindy's pace. 'Mr Chapman didn't seem that keen on any kind of computer interference.'

'Do either of you have a better plan?' Cindy demanded, deliberately not looking their way.

'Well, no, but—'

'I think George and Miss Sinclair are just worried this might all go wrong, like Sam said,' Leah interrupted. She was trailing behind because of her knee; it was aching dully with every step.

'Especially the bit where he told us we might accidentally blow up the rocket.'

Cindy didn't answer. Instead, she just walked quicker, turning the corner and almost smacking into the chest of a security guard. It was the same guard who had caught them in the control room last time. Leah saw his eyes light with recognition.

'What are you kids doing?' he snarled. 'Didn't I already tell you that you couldn't be here?'

'You don't understand,' Cindy panted. 'We need to—'

'There's a Soviet spy tied up in an office down there!' Mimi burst out, pointing the way they'd just come.

The guard's face twitched with alarm, and for a second Leah thought that Mimi's bluff might work, but then his face shuttered, his expression becoming harsh.

'Nice try,' he spat. 'But I'm not falling for that! Don't you know this is an important day? Buzz off before I call back-up and have you all hauled outta here.'

Cindy opened her mouth to argue, but before

she could, Miss Sinclair marched her way to the front. The security guard's face twitched with surprise.

'Miss Sinclair!' he said. 'I didn't see you there.'

'Yes, well, it's no problem,' Miss Sinclair said, using the same authoritative voice she'd used with Sam. 'If you could just let us in there . . .' She gestured towards the door.

But the security guard shook his head again, looking chagrined. 'I'm sorry, ma'am, but Mr Whistler said no one in or out until the launch is complete. Today's take-off is closed to spectators.'

Suddenly, a voice echoed through the door. *'Attention! T minus thirty-five minutes until take-off. All engineers assume positions!'*

Leah's expression was panic-stricken as she stared at her friends. They needed to get inside that room!

Miss Sinclair had been distracted by the announcement, but now she inhaled sharply, her eyebrows climbing so high they nearly disappeared into her hair. She turned back to the security guard, her face fierce. 'Spectators? Excuse me! I am his assistant. The director will *absolutely* want me in there!'

But the security guard was immovable. 'He said he'd have my job if I disobeyed him.'

His reply didn't please Miss Sinclair. Her expression became dark and stormy.

Cindy was positively vibrating with impatience and she opened her mouth to speak, but Leah grabbed her arm, pulling her away as Miss Sinclair and the security guard began to argue in earnest.

'What are you doing?' Cindy hissed.

'Getting creative!' Leah responded. She backed away slowly and tugged Cindy into a side room. Her friends followed behind. George craned his neck around the door frame to see if either the security guard or Miss Sinclair had noticed their disappearance, but after a second he shook his head and shut the door quietly behind him.

'They're too busy trying to prove who's right,' he said, striding into the centre of the room and leaning against a desk. Mimi began to wander around, her gaze running over the walls.

'But my mom . . . !' Cindy began.

'We're still going to help her,' Leah said. 'But that guard wasn't going to let us through.'

'And at least we've got rid of Miss Sinclair,' Mimi offered.

Cindy spun away, tugging on her plaits angrily. 'Argh! I need to get into that room! We're running out of time!'

'Are there any other entrances?' George asked.

'No,' Cindy answered. 'That guard is blocking the only way in.' She sounded like she was trying not to cry.

'Hey,' Mimi suddenly piped up. 'I know how we can get in.'

'You do?' Leah raised her eyebrow. 'How?'

'Through there,' Mimi replied, pointing to the ceiling.

Leah looked up.

In the middle of the ceiling was a grate about the same size as a large pizza box. There were four screws, one at each corner, holding it in place.

'The vents?' George choked out. 'You want us to climb through the ventilation system?'

'Why not?' Mimi said. 'We're running out of options, and besides, they always do it in the movies!'

George groaned.

Leah, however, was already thinking about how they'd get up there. The ceilings weren't that high. If they pushed a desk underneath the grate, they might *just* be able to reach.

'Come on,' she said, pushing George off the desk he was leaning on. 'Help me get this into position.'

'L!' George's eyes goggled in disbelief. 'You can't be serious!'

'Mimi's right. We don't have any other options and you heard what Sam said. There's probably only thirty minutes left until launch! If we don't get into that room, Intrepid Two is going to take off with Nancy inside and we won't be able to save her.' She broke off. She didn't say what else she was thinking: that if they didn't get in that room and save Nancy, they would have failed the watch's mission and they'd never be able to get home.

George's eyes widened as he understood what Leah wasn't saying. He swallowed audibly and then rushed to her side, bracing himself against the desk. Mimi and Cindy joined them, and together, inch by inch, they managed to push it underneath the vent.

Mindful of her knee, Leah clambered up first. She inspected the screws, trying to turn them with her fingers, but they were stuck fast.

She puffed out a breath of annoyance. 'I can't get it open,' she said.

'Wait!' Cindy said. 'I have just the thing to open those screws!' With a flourish, she produced her screwdriver from her pocket. Marty's head poked out and he squeaked.

'Quick, Leah! Swap with me,' Cindy instructed.

Leah scooted down off the desk and helped Cindy up. Her friend stuck her tongue out as she concentrated on the grate. With steady hands, she fitted the end of the screwdriver into the screw and began to twist.

'Ugh!' she grunted. 'Someone did these up tight!' Cindy gritted her teeth, gripping the screwdriver as hard as she could. Eventually, there came a squeal and the first screw came loose, spinning swiftly out of the vent and clattering to the floor.

'Yes!' Leah breathed as Cindy moved on to the next. One after the other, they *plunk*ed down beside the first. 'Cindy, that was so cool!'

'Yeah, yeah, let's just open this vent and you can all be amazed later,' Cindy replied, pocketing her screwdriver, but Leah thought she looked quite pleased with herself.

'Right,' Leah said, nodding. She clambered up next to Cindy, and together they tugged at the grate until it came loose with a low metallic *skreeeek*. Leah threw it down onto the carpet alongside the screws.

The dark entrance to the vents loomed above.

Leah felt her hands begin to shake as nerves stirred inside her, but she squashed them down as hard as she could. She didn't have time to be nervous. Nancy was relying on them. They *had* to do this.

Praying that her knee was strong enough,

Leah gripped the edge of the opening and hauled herself up.

She panted, her arms trembling as she fought to pull her body into the vent. For a moment, she hung suspended, her legs kicking fiercely as she tried to get a better grip.

And then there were hands on her feet, pushing her upwards.

She looked down to see that George and Mimi had climbed onto the desk alongside Cindy and they were lifting her up.

It was the boost she needed. Fingers scrambling, Leah managed to hook her uninjured knee over the left edge of the grate and flop inside. She was panting hard.

'L, give Cindy your hand!' George called.

Leah turned round on her knees and stuck her head back over the rim of the grate. She reached out her hand and Cindy gripped it hard. Leah pulled and George and Mimi pushed, heaving until Cindy popped over onto the right-hand side.

Mimi went next, and then it was George's turn, and soon all four of them were collapsed on the cold metal floor of the vent.

'The movies always make that look much easier,' Mimi mused as they waited for George to catch his breath.

'Come on,' said Cindy, turning around on her knees so that she was facing into the gloom. 'I think it's this way.'

Mimi followed her, with George going next, and Leah edging around the open vent and bringing up the rear.

The ventilation system was dark, dusty and very cramped. The dust tickled Leah's nose and she fought the urge to sneeze. In the distance, they could see other grates, small squares of light piercing the darkness. But there wasn't much they could do about the restricted space. In fact, they'd only gone a few metres before the duct became even smaller. Leah and her friends had no choice but to slide forward on their bellies, pushing themselves forward with their arms and their knees. Marty squeezed himself out of Cindy's pocket and perched on her shoulder, hunkering down so that he wouldn't be squashed against the top of the duct.

'This is such a bad idea,' George wheezed from in front of Leah.

'Relax, George,' Mimi huffed. 'We won't be in here for much longer.'

'Relax? Relax? I'm claustrophobic, scared of the dark and I don't like heights. How exactly am I supposed to relax?' It sounded like George's breaths were coming faster and faster.

Leah tried to make her voice as soothing as possible. 'It's okay. We're all with you and we're going to get through this.'

'Why is this taking so long?' he groaned, as if she hadn't spoken.

Suddenly, Cindy stopped ahead of them. 'Oh,' she said. 'Oh no.'

'What do you mean, *Oh no*?' George's voice was getting louder.

'Shh, George, they'll hear you!' Leah hissed. 'Cindy, what's the problem?'

'This is the right vent, but . . . it's screwed in, too, and the screws are on the other side. We can't get through!' Cindy's voice was edged with panic.

'Do you mean . . . ?' George's voice trembled. 'Do you mean we're stuck in here?'

'No,' Leah said quickly. 'I'm sure that's not what Cindy meant at all. Let me through and I'll have a look. Maybe the key can help us get out.'

She edged forward, trying to slip around

George, but the duct was even narrower than she'd thought. There wasn't enough room for the two of them.

'Ouch!' George yelped as Leah's foot slammed into his leg. 'Watch out!'

'Sorry,' Leah huffed. 'If you could just *breathe* in, maybe I could get past.'

'Wait, no, why don't we move back first?' Mimi suggested. She began to reverse. The heel of her shoe collided with Leah's nose and Leah reared back. Beneath her, the floor of the vent creaked.

'Ah!' Leah yelped. 'Stop!'

'Guys, can you hear that?' Cindy said from up ahead, but the others weren't listening to her.

'Sorry, L!' Mimi said sheepishly.

'George, why don't you try to shuffle back?' Leah suggested.

'Because you're squashing me!' George complained, but he began to wiggle, his body banging against the duct wall.

'Guys!' Cindy shouted, and it was the note of panic in her voice that finally made Leah stop. 'Listen!'

There was an unhappy groan from all around them. Leah gasped as the base of the vent rolled. Her fingers scrabbled for purchase, but there was nothing for her to grip onto, just smooth metal. An awful grinding sound crashed through the narrow vent, and then Leah was dropping, her stomach lurching up into her throat. As the duct gave way beneath their weight, Leah and her friends tumbled through the hole, their limbs flailing as bits of dust, metal and ceiling rained down with them.

CHAPTER 25: T MINUS FIVE MINUTES

For a moment, Leah lay dazed, blinking frantically through the haze of dust. It settled on her eyelashes like snow. Her mouth was dry and her heart was jumping. There was a painful throbbing around her knee.

Leah, Mimi, George and Cindy had all landed in a heap, surrounded by bits of warped metal vent and battered ceiling tiles. Leah caught a flash of a mouse's tail darting over Cindy's shoulder and was relieved that Marty seemed to be okay.

But her relief was short-lived.

As the dust cleared, she saw that Cindy had been right. They *had* found the vent into the control room, and now there were more than a dozen pairs of bewildered eyes staring at them. It seemed that their dramatic entrance had gathered quite an audience. The door to the control room crashed open as the security guard from outside rushed in. Behind him was Miss Sinclair. She stared at the children in shock.

'What on earth is going on?' roared a familiar voice, and the crowd shuffled and mumbled as a figure fought its way to the front.

It was Mr Whistler, and when he saw them, he stopped abruptly, his eyes going wide. His mouth flopped open.

Mr Jones appeared at his shoulder, and whilst the director of the NACA seemed to be speechless, the lead engineer took one look at the tangle of children on the control room floor and knew exactly what to say. His face turned purply-puce with anger and he barked, 'Security!'

Leah's head was still ringing from the fall and she felt a bit dizzy, but she disentangled her legs from George's and pushed herself to her feet. Her knee protested and she shifted her weight to ease the pressure. She wanted to sit down, but there wasn't any time. Who knew how long they'd been crawling through that vent? The launch could happen at any moment!

'No!' she cried as the security guard began to advance towards them. 'Wait! We need to stop that rocket!'

She pointed her finger at the big screen on the far wall. It displayed an image of a white rocket gleaming under the Florida sun. Only a couple of days ago, Leah had stood in this exact spot and watched its twin be consumed in a fiery blaze.

Mr Jones snorted. 'This is ridiculous,' he said

dismissively. He glared at the security guard. 'Will you *please* get these children out of here and call their mothers?'

'But my mother is in *there*!' Cindy protested, jumping up to stand by Leah.

Mr Jones blinked. He looked at the screen. 'What are you talking about?'

'She's in that rocket!' Cindy's eyes were wide.

There were a few awkward titters as the room fell silent at Cindy's words. Mr Jones's face was contorted in an expression that was half furious and half disbelieving.

'How dare you—' the lead engineer began, his brows lowered.

'It's true!' Leah interrupted. 'She really is in there. If you don't believe us, you can call Sam Chapman. He's in Cape Canaveral and he'll tell you! But we're running out of time!'

'You need to let me onto one of those computers,' Cindy said, jabbing her finger at one of the units closest to her. The man sitting at it jumped, moving towards the keyboard as if to protect it. 'I can stop the launch.'

'She's telling the truth!' a voice called from the door, and Leah turned to see Miss Sinclair striding forward, her face determined. 'Please, Edward—'

But Mr Jones wasn't listening. 'That is *enough*!' he bellowed, throwing his hands in the air. 'I don't know what you think you're playing at, Miss Sinclair, but now is not the time for it! Neither you nor these *children* have any business being in this room, and I won't stand for it. You need to leave! Right, sir? Sir?' He turned to Mr Whistler, but the director said nothing. His eyes were swivelling between Miss Sinclair and the children, his face drained of colour.

'But . . . but it's not a lie! My mom really is in there,' Cindy sputtered. She pointed at Mr Whistler. '*He* put her in there. She found out something about a technical fault and budget cuts, and he didn't want anyone to know, so he kidnapped her.'

Mr Jones glared at Cindy. 'Why, you little liar!' he hissed. He beckoned at the guard once again.

Leah began to panic. This was their only opportunity to save Nancy. But she knew that convincing Mr Jones that they were telling the truth was going to be nearly impossible. They needed to try another angle.

'If you don't listen to us,' she shouted, 'that rocket is going to explode again, and then you'll *never* beat the Soviet Union. Mr Whistler told you all that the last launch failed because of a maths problem, but that wasn't true. It was actually a problem with the navigation system. If you just wait and take a look, you'll see! But if you launch that rocket now, it's going to go badly wrong.'

'What nonsense,' Mr Jones scoffed. 'Our reports don't say anything about a faulty navigation system and Mr Whistler personally looked over Nancy's notes himself and told me the numbers were incorrect—'

'No,' Mimi said, squaring her shoulders and lifting her chin. 'Her notes had been tampered with. The calculations were never the problem – the faulty navigation system was.'

'It's true,' Miss Sinclair interjected. She stared at the floor, her cheeks aflame. 'I . . . I'm the one who changed Nancy's calculations because *he* told me to! Intrepid One exploded because of a technical issue. Not a mathematical one!' She looked up and pointed a quivering finger at Mr Whistler. Around her, the room seemed to take a disbelieving breath.

'You were convinced the fault was a one-off accident and you didn't want to spend time proving it, so you needed something to blame, didn't you, Mr Whistler? Something that could be fixed quickly,' Mimi continued with narrowed eyes. 'Especially because the only reason there was a problem in the first place was because you'd been cutting corners and trying to save money. The budget cuts have made things difficult for you. Mr Jones, you should know about that too, especially because Sam tried to tell you he didn't have enough staff to get Intrepid Two ready. He tried to warn you all. Don't you see? Nancy's calculations were never the problem, they were just the cover-up. Miss Sinclair stole them and erased the original numbers, inserting incorrect ones over the top so you'd all think they were the cause. Show them, George.'

George dug the papers from where he'd stashed them in his jeans pocket and held them out to Mr Jones. The lead engineer took them, his nose wrinkled with distaste. But then his eyes widened as he noted the different handwriting.

'Didn't you all stop to wonder why the best mathematician in Langley had made such a glaring error?' Mimi demanded, her eyes glowing. 'Since we've arrived, all we've heard is how well-respected Nancy Grant is and how thorough her calculations are. Maybe it was because she's a woman that you were so quick to trust the word of the man in charge over hers. But it turns out that the man in charge is the problem. He's so desperate to win and beat the Soviets that Mr Whistler is willing to do anything and everything he can, instead of taking the time and having the patience to make sure it's all done correctly.'

For a beat, no one spoke. Leah felt pride rush through her as she stared at Mimi. Maybe it was her acting skills coming through, but Leah had never seen her friend speak so passionately. The entire room seemed as though it were under her spell.

And then a hard, cruel laugh shattered it.

Mr Whistler took a step towards them, finally breaking free of the trance that had held him captive. 'Goodness,' he said, a benevolent smile on his face. 'What overactive imaginations you all have! I have to admit, I've always had my doubts about women working in the sciences, but I thought it was only fair they had their chance, even if hiring both them and Black people went against my better judgement. And now look where we are! Just like Nancy, you little girls are far too hysterical to think as rationally and logically as men do. And we have no room for hysterics in the space programme.' His gaze flashed to Miss Sinclair, his eyes hard. The PA seemed to wilt under his scrutiny. 'I'm especially disappointed in you, Irene. I gave you so many chances to be a part of what we're trying to achieve here.' He shook his head, his features twisted in pity.

Leah felt a sense of dread sweep over her as she saw that the engineers in the room, including Mr Jones, were listening to him. Some of them were even nodding.

But suddenly, Miss Sinclair straightened, and anger rolled across her features. She glowered at the NACA director. 'No, Mr Whistler,' she spat. 'Women aren't the problem here. *You* are, and you're not going to get away with this.' Before anyone could move, she lunged towards the nearest desk, snatching up the phone. Her fingers danced on the wheel, spinning it as she put the correct number in. 'We have proof.'

'Stop her and get these children out of here!' Mr Whistler bellowed.

'Hello, Sam? It's Irene Sinclair. I'm going to need a favour. That internal camera you're looking at, the one showing Nancy Grant trapped inside Intrepid Two? Can you patch it through to Mission Control here at Langley?' She paused, and then swivelled to face Mr Whistler, her eyes narrowed in suspicion. 'Oh, you've been trying to get through to Mission Control but all the lines are jammed? How interesting. I think someone might be interfering with the communication equipment.' Leah wasn't sure how, but Mr Whistler must have been blocking incoming calls to the control room. 'Well, I'm in here now and they're all very eager to see what you can see. Great, thank you.'

Miss Sinclair put the receiver down, and as she did, the huge screen on the far wall flickered. The footage of the rocket standing on the launch pad vanished. In its place, another image appeared. It showed what was very clearly the *inside* of a rocket. The panelled walls were a mixture of white and grey, with strange dials and monitors dotted here and there. Pipes ran up and down the tube-like interior and, handcuffed to one of them, was Nancy Grant.

Cindy made a whimpering sound as a gasp ran through the room. Nancy was slumped against the pipe, still wearing the clothes she'd been in on Wednesday. Her eyes were closed and her head was tipped back against the wall. There was a nasty bruise above her eyebrow.

A heavy silence filled the room. Some people were staring at Mr Whistler, and others were staring at the rocket. There was a choked sound as someone started to cry.

'Is this really true, Robert?' Mr Jones said, his voice quiet. 'Did you . . . did you do this?'

'Of course, not!' Mr Whistler scoffed, but his eyes were darting frantically left and right, like a rat trying to find a way out of a trap.

'It's worse than that,' George piped up. 'Not only did he kidnap her, but he planned to get rid of her once and for all. He knows that even if that rocket launches successfully, it won't make it back down to Earth in one piece. It'll explode, taking Nancy with it.'

'Robert, how could you?' Mr Jones cried, appalled. 'Our entire life's work . . . it's all about freedom and pushing the boundaries of the known world. And you would . . . you planned to . . .' The lead engineer squeezed his eyes shut and shuddered. Leah almost felt sorry for him. 'How long have we got until take-off?' Mr Jones demanded, turning away from his boss.

An engineer answered, his voice shaking. 'T minus five minutes.'

Leah felt her stomach sink. What were they going to do? Surely that wouldn't be enough time to hack the computers and get Nancy free!

She was so focused on their predicament that she didn't see the shift on Mr Whistler's face. He set his jaw, his expression determined, then darted forward. At first, Leah thought he was trying to run for the door, but instead he swiped a remote control up from a desk. He held it out before him, his hand shaking, his thumb poised over a big red button.

'Nobody move!' he screamed, his eyes wild. 'If . . . if you do, if you get even *one* step closer to me, I'm going to press this button and launch that rocket immediately!'

CHAPTER 26: SEVEN SECONDS

Miss Sinclair gasped and Leah froze. Next to her, Mimi, George and Cindy had all gone rigid as they stared at Mr Whistler and the big red button he was seconds away from pressing. Her mouth felt dry, her hands clammy. She swallowed and it sounded so loud to her own ears that she was surprised no one else could hear it.

'You don't understand,' spat the director of the NACA, his gaze swinging erratically between them. 'None of you do! The pressure I'm under . . . it's all-consuming! When Nancy found out what had *really* happened . . . I couldn't let her tell anyone!'

'So you kidnapped her,' Leah said.

Mr Whistler's mouth turned up into a sneer.

'It was too easy. I left like I always do, but then I pulled my car up near the West Computing Area. When Nancy came across the compound, it was a simple thing to pretend I was having car trouble and shove her inside. Then, a quick drive to hand her off to my associates, who delivered her to Cape Canaveral overnight.' He cackled, and Leah shuddered at the coldness in his voice. 'She couldn't see my vision. *None* of you do! The President . . . he understands. He wants what I want – for America to be the best, to be the winner. But he doesn't understand what I need to get us there and what he's asking of me . . . it's too much! The White House is cutting my funding, and running the NACA like I used to is impossible.'

'But . . .' Leah's tongue darted out, licking her lips. 'But surely the President knows that. He can't expect you to—'

'Yes he can!' Mr Whistler roared, his shout cutting Leah off. 'He can and he does. He's . . . disappointed with me. With me and with the NACA.' He paused, pursing his lips. 'I've heard the rumours. Rumours that he's going to get rid of this organization and replace it with something new. Something *better*. "NASA" they're calling it.' Mr Whistler gave a cold, humourless laugh. 'And I know how these things happen. I'm not stupid! They'll set this NASA up and the whole department will be reshuffled. Out with the old and in with the new. Well, I'm not going to let them throw *me* out. I'm going to do whatever it takes to make sure I keep my office, and if I have to cut a thousand corners and blow up hundreds of rockets and *kidnap* tens of meddling mathematicians before I show this country what I'm made of, I will!'

Leah felt a cold snake of horror coil through her. Mr Whistler really meant it. She could see it in his eyes. He knew that Intrepid Two was going to fail, but he didn't care. He only saw it as a means to an end. A way to get rid of Nancy and show the President that the NACA was still working towards beating the Soviet Union. That's why he was so impatient to launch the next rocket and ready to throw caution to the wind. The successful Soviet Union launch the day before had made him panic. He wanted the United States to win, but he only wanted it to happen if he was the one in charge.

Something in Mr Whistler's expression shifted, and the thumb that he'd been hovering over the red button stopped shaking. His lips were thin with determination and Leah's heart lurched.

He was going to press the button and launch Nancy to her doom.

Leah lunged forward, desperate to stop him.

But before she could, Mr Whistler froze, his eyes going wide. He made a noise that sounded similar to a squeak and then he stuck his left leg out and began to shake it.

'Ah! Ah!' he cried. 'What is that? Get it off me!'

Leah looked at her friends, bewildered.

Mr Whistler's body was jerking and dancing around like a puppet on a string. Then, with an almighty roar, he thrust his leg out one final time and a tiny shape flew out of the bottom of his suit leg and through the air, landing on the floor in front of Mimi. It was Marty! She scooped him up just as Mr Whistler gave a triumphant shout.

'Ha!' he shouted, the remote still held firmly in his hand. But Marty had distracted him for just enough time . . .

There was a sudden high-pitched 'HY-AAAHH!' and Mr Jones tipped his body, his right leg coming up in a powerful side kick that knocked the remote from Mr Whistler's hands. It tumbled through the air until it came to land on

the floor by the door. An engineer scrambled to pick it up, staring at it as if it were an unexploded bomb.

Mr Whistler's eyes flared in shock, but he didn't get the chance to move even an inch because Mr Jones was already on him, clasping his hands behind his back and holding them steady whilst the security guard rushed over.

'Hold him until we've sorted this,' Mr Jones told the guard. He looked at Mr Whistler with disgust.

Mr Whistler barely noticed. He was struggling, trying to prise himself free, but it was no use. The security guard's hands were like iron.

Mr Jones shook his head. 'I'll call the police when I'm done.'

'That was so impressive!' George gasped as Mr Jones turned his attention to them.

Mr Jones gave a careless shrug. 'I've got some experience with martial arts,' he told them. Leah remembered the karate certificates they'd seen in his office.

'Sir,' Cindy interrupted. 'We need to save my

mom! Time's running out!'

'Right.' Mr Jones nodded. He turned to one of the computer operators. 'How long have we got?'

'Launch is T minus two minutes, sir,' the operator replied.

'This computer has a link to the rocket's computer systems,' Mr Jones told Cindy, indicating a terminal on the end of the row. 'What are you thinking?'

Cindy jumped into action immediately, sliding into the desk chair and tapping away at the keyboard. 'We need to initiate a launch-pad abort.'

Mr Jones paled, his lips pressed into a thin, disapproving line. 'But . . . doing that remotely is extremely difficult. You'll only have—'

Cindy interrupted him. 'Seven seconds. I know.' Her forehead was furrowed in concentration as she clicked through a series of windows on the screen.

'Are you sure you have the experience to—'

'Sir, Cindy probably knows more about science and computers than you do,' George interrupted.

'She's really good at this stuff.'

Mr Jones didn't look convinced, but Cindy's voice was solid as she said, 'I can do it. My mom is on that rocket. I *have* to do it.'

'But—'

'Look.' Cindy paused, swivelling in her chair to pin Mr Jones with a glare. 'You can either be quiet and let me work, or you can help me out. Which is it going to be?'

Mr Jones looked torn, but then he sighed. 'I'm going to help you, of course,' he muttered, pulling out the chair next to hers.

Leah, Mimi and George lingered behind Cindy's shoulder, watching as she worked. The screen was black, with a series of blinking green numbers appearing in horizontal lines. Cindy spoke as she worked, her fingers a blur as they moved across the keyboard.

'First I need to override the rocket's computers,' she said. 'That won't take too long. Aha! We're in. Now, I just need to scramble the code so that the rocket registers a fault.'

'T minus one minute!' the operator cried. On

the screen, Nancy stirred, her eyes fluttering as the rocket around her began to hum.

'A faulty sensor would do it,' Mr Jones said urgently. 'That would indicate abnormal fuel flow and trigger an automatic abort.'

'Nice,' Cindy said with an approving nod. Rivulets of sweat dripped down her neck and her entire body was trembling.

Leah could almost hear the *tick-tock* of the clock working against them.

'I'm almost there . . .' Cindy whispered. Mr Jones's fists were curled into tight coils.

'T minus ten seconds!'

Leah wanted to look away but she couldn't. Her entire body felt like jelly and her gaze jumped from Cindy's computer to the footage of Nancy on the big screen.

Suddenly, the shrill ringing of a phone shattered the tense silence and Leah jumped. Somebody answered it.

'It's Mr Chapman,' an engineer called in a frantic voice. Vaguely, Leah realized someone must have unblocked the phone lines. 'He said the three main engines on the orbiter have engaged. You have—'

'Seven seconds!' Leah, George and Mimi cried.

'I know!' Cindy shouted at the same time.

Her fingers moved so quickly that Leah could barely follow them. Lines of script appeared and disappeared, the numbers whirling together and sending commands to the rocket on the screen. Leah's mouth was hanging open, her heart beating so fast that she swore it would explode from her chest at any moment.

Four . . .

Three . . .

Two . . .

Cindy slammed one finger down onto a final key and spun her chair away from the desk. 'I'm done! I'm done!' she cried.

Someone, somewhere, shouted, 'Lift-off!'

Leah's breath hitched unevenly in her chest as she stared at the rocket. She waited for the roaring flames. For the explosion.

It didn't come.

The rocket didn't move.

'Did it work? Is she safe?' Cindy demanded, eyes bright.

The engineer was still on the phone and they stared at him, the silence thickening like treacle.

Finally, he turned to them, his mouth agape. 'You did it!' he whispered. Then louder, 'He said you did it! The orbiter engines have powered down! The rocket isn't going to launch.'

Cindy let out a sound that was half-laugh and half-sob, folding over so that her head was resting on her chest. Leah threw her arms around her, squeezing tight, relief filling her body. After a second, Mimi and George joined her.

Around them, the control room was in a frenzy. Mr Jones was pacing up and down, issuing instructions about cooling operations and stabilizing fuel chambers, but Leah and her friends barely heard any of it.

All they heard was the engineer on the phone as he said, 'They're going to get her now. They're going to get Nancy out.'

CHAPTER 27: CRASH, BANG, SPLUTTER

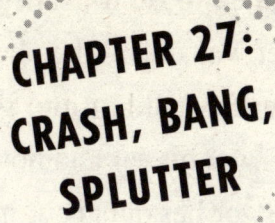

The children stayed huddled together whilst the adults buzzed around them. There was an air of giddiness in the room, as if everyone were so relieved that all sense of seriousness had disappeared. But there was one person who wasn't happy.

Mr Whistler glowered at everyone, his hands still held fast by the security guard. He looked angry, but also a little nervous. He'd confessed everything to a room full of people, and now the police were on their way to collect statements and take him into custody. There was no way for him to talk his way out of this one.

Leah felt a sense of satisfaction. She was glad he was going to be punished, especially after what he'd planned to do to Nancy.

The engineer was still on the phone to Sam, and Leah could see him talking into the receiver. He pulled it away from his ear and now called over to them. 'They've got her out! Your mom is safe!'

Cindy had already been crying before, but now her sobs grew even louder. Leah, Mimi and George looked at each other, grinning wildly.

Suddenly, there was a loud shout.

Leah spun around just in time to see Mr Whistler break free of the security guard, yanking his hands away with tremendous strength. His teeth were bared in a grimace of rage. Pushing the guard aside, he barrelled his way through the room and out into the corridor.

'No!' Mr Jones cried. 'Don't let him get away!'

Leah jumped up and set off in pursuit, careering out into the hallway and following the director down the hallway. But she didn't get very far before her injured knee began to complain, sending painful protests up and down her leg. She hissed, hopping to a halt. Mimi drew up beside her, her face a mask of concern.

Leah waved her off. 'Don't worry about me!' she cried. 'Just go after him! I'll catch you up!'

Mimi nodded and sprinted off towards the foyer, with George and Cindy behind her. Mr Jones and the security guard were following close on their heels.

Growling with frustration, Leah limped after them. She didn't rush, though. If there was one thing she'd learned today, rushing something before it was ready only ended in disaster.

By the time she'd hobbled across the foyer and pushed her way through the glass doors, Mimi, George and Cindy were all standing on the pavement, staring out over the car park. Mr Jones and the security guard stood either side of Mr Whistler's beat-up blue estate car, banging on the windows. The director was inside, wrestling with the handbrake.

Suddenly, there was a *pop* and a *bang*, and Mr Whistler's car sputtered to life, the exhaust pipe coughing black smoke. Behind the steering wheel, Leah saw him smile triumphantly as he put the car in reverse and zoomed backwards.

He jerked the steering wheel around, roaring off towards the exit. Leah's heart plummeted.

But then the car gave an alarming judder, the bonnet beginning to shake. With a high-pitched squeal, Mr Whistler's car came to a halt on the tarmac. She could see him beating at the steering wheel and yanking on the gears, but it was no use. His car wasn't going anywhere.

'Look!' Mimi shouted, pointing in the opposite direction to Mr Whistler's car. 'Who's that?'

Leah pivoted to see two figures racing across the car park. She gasped as she recognized them as the two mysterious people she'd seen hanging around the other day.

She'd thought they were Soviet spies, but as they skidded to a stop outside Mr Whistler's car and forced the doors open, she could see that she'd been very wrong. They wielded black badges in their hands and were shouting, 'FBI, FBI! Put your hands on your head!'

Leah and her friends watched in surprise as the FBI agents dragged Mr Whistler from his car, but before they could get a proper grip on him, the NACA director pushed them both away with a desperate roar. He dodged forward, trying to make a run for it.

Out of the corner of her eye, Leah saw a golden blur rush past.

It was Apollo! The old dog had his lips drawn back in a snarl as he bounded towards Mr Whistler. With a loud bark, he leapt towards the director's fleeing back, planting his paws between his shoulder blades. Mr Whistler gave a shout of surprise as he stumbled, and then tripped, falling face-first onto the tarmac.

'Yes, Apollo!' Mimi shouted, thrusting her fist into the air.

Within seconds, the FBI agents had surrounded Mr Whistler. Apollo jumped away and the two men dragged the director up, twisting him round and pushing him against the side of the car. Rust flaked off, smearing his smart suit with orange streaks. The agents clapped handcuffs around Mr Whistler's wrists.

'We've been watching you very closely, Mr Whistler,' one of them said. 'I'm so glad we've

finally got to meet in person.'

The second agent noticed that they had an audience and strode over to where the children were stood. Mr Jones and the security guard had joined them.

'Howdy, folks,' he said. His smile was kind, and he had a deep accent that reminded Leah of the cowboy films her grandpa liked to watch. 'Are you all acquainted with Mr Whistler?'

Mr Jones grimaced. 'Unfortunately. We've just found out that he kidnapped one of our mathematicians and tried to blow her up in a rocket.'

The agent's eyes went wide and he gave a low whistle. 'Gee, is that so? Well, we've got warrants for his arrest due to charges of fraud and embezzlement.'

'Fraud and embezzle-what?' Mimi said, raising her eyebrows.

The FBI agent smiled. 'It means that Mr Whistler here has been telling some big lies and stealing money from the NACA for his own use.'

George's mouth hung open in shock. 'Does that mean he's going to prison?'

'Yes, sir,' the FBI agent replied. 'And now with kidnapping and attempted murder added to his charges, well, that man is in a whole heap of trouble.'

'It was my mom he tried to hurt,' Cindy said, her trembling hands curled into tight fists.

The FBI agent quirked an eyebrow. 'Would you be willing to give me a statement about that, little miss?' he asked.

Cindy sent a withering glare in Mr Whistler's direction. 'If it'll help put him in prison for a long time, I'd be happy to.'

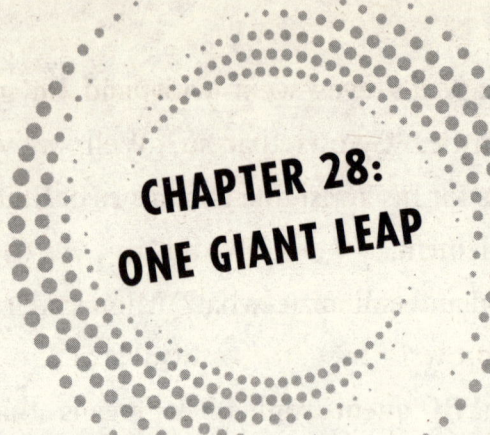

CHAPTER 28: ONE GIANT LEAP

Exhausted, the children slumped down on the stairs leading up to the front door of the Aeronautics building. One of the FBI agents had collected statements from them, whilst the other had bundled Mr Whistler, thrashing and shouting, into the back of their car. At some point, a police car had whined to a halt in the car park, and now uniformed bodies were striding through the crowd that had gathered, asking questions.

'Look!' Mimi suddenly shouted, pointing behind them at the door to the Aeronautics building. A security guard had emerged, and next to him was Miss Sinclair. She saw the children and headed over to them.

'You did it,' she said, grinning. 'You saved

your mom, Cindy, and you stopped the rocket from launching! You're heroes, all of you!'

Cindy rubbed the back of her head, looking sheepish. 'Yeah, I guess we did. But we couldn't have done it without you.'

George nodded enthusiastically. 'They never would have believed us.'

'You know...' Cindy began to say, but then she trailed off, thinking hard. 'You know, the police don't have to know you helped Mr Whistler. We don't have to tell them.'

But Miss Sinclair shook her head and smiled gently. 'No, it's too late for that, I'm afraid. Everyone in that control room heard me say I'd tampered with your mom's notes. Besides, actions have consequences, and now I need to live with mine.' Her American flag on her collar twinkled in the sunlight as she patted Cindy on the shoulder. Taking a big breath, Miss Sinclair drew her shoulders back, gave a firm nod and then strode off to where the FBI agents were standing.

Leah watched as she spoke to the men. They nodded, and then one of them led her to their car. She slid inside and, after a moment, both the police car and the FBI car drove away, taking the prisoners with them.

It was over.

'I can't believe we did it,' said Mimi softly.

George shuddered. 'When Mr Whistler was holding that remote, I was sure he was going to launch the rocket.'

Cindy had been silent, but now she took a big breath. 'I just wish it had been anyone but him. Do you know that Mr Whistler and my mom have worked together for almost as long as I've been alive? I thought... I thought we meant something to him.' Her face was carved with sadness.

Leah reached over and took her hand, squeezing it. 'I'm sure in his own way, you *did* mean something to him. But, in the end, winning – and money – meant more.'

'And you, Cindy... you were fantastic!' George gushed. 'I knew you were good with computers and all that technical stuff, but I didn't realize you were *that* good!'

Mimi nodded enthusiastically. 'Without you,

we never would have been able to save your mum.'

'You're going to make an amazing engineer one day,' Leah said, grinning.

Cindy ducked her head, her mouth twisted into a sheepish smile. 'Thanks, guys.'

'You know what's going to be even better than saving the day, though?' George said, leaning back and stretching his arms above his head. 'Seeing your mum's face when we tell her about it!'

Leah, Mimi and Cindy burst out laughing. Marty poked his head out of Cindy's pocket, squeaking enthusiastically.

Suddenly, Leah's entire body jerked, as if she'd been hit by a bolt of lightning. Her neck was hot. And it was getting hotter! She gasped as she realized what was happening, her hand flying up to the chain hidden underneath her collar. She fished the watch out, holding it before her.

'What time is it?' she asked urgently.

Cindy looked puzzled. 'Probably about lunchtime?'

Leah looked at Mimi and George. Their faces were full of understanding as they both stared at the watch. They'd done what they'd set out to do, and now it was time to finally go home.

'It looks like we won't be here to tell Nancy about what happened after all,' Leah said with a sad smile. Whenever the watch brought them back to the past, she was always eager to complete their mission so that they could get back to the future. But when the time came, all she felt was sadness. Leah hated leaving her new friends behind.

'What do you mean?' Cindy asked, raising an eyebrow. Marty clambered out of her pocket, scurrying up to perch on her shoulder. He tilted his little head to one side, his whiskers twitching inquisitively. 'Do you mean you have to get back to the space camp?'

Mimi laughed, her eyes bright. 'Cindy, come on. You didn't *really* believe we were part of the space camp, did you? Don't you think our teachers would have been looking for us?'

Cindy's mouth dropped open, and she sputtered, trying to find a response. In the end, all she could say was, 'Well, where are you from, then?'

Leah looked at George and Mimi, a question

lighting her eyes. Mimi shrugged and, after a beat, George nodded.

'It's a bit complicated, but, basically, we're from the future,' Leah said.

Cindy gaped at them, and then she snorted. 'Nice try, guys, but I'm not going to fall for that.'

'It's true,' Mimi insisted. 'That watch Leah's holding is another one of our magic items, and it takes us back in time.'

'You mean . . . it's like the key and the magnifying glass?' Cindy said slowly. Leah could see her brain whirring as she tried to understand what they were telling her.

'Exactly.' Leah nodded. Cindy still didn't look convinced.

George sighed in exasperation. 'We're literally sat outside a building that only exists to try to launch a person *into space*!' he said. 'If we can do that, then why wouldn't we be able to travel through time, too?'

Cindy tilted her head to the side. 'Huh. Well, I guess that makes sense.'

The watch suddenly grew even hotter in Leah's

palm and she looked at her friends. 'It's time,' she told them. 'We've got to go now, or we'll miss our window. Grab hold of me.'

George threaded one of his arms through Leah's, and Mimi did the same on the other side. Leah took a deep breath, hovering her finger over the watch's crown.

'Wait!' Cindy said, leaning forward. 'Does this mean . . . Will I ever see you again?'

Leah shook her head. 'I don't know,' she said. 'Maybe one day.'

'We're running out of time, L,' Mimi said urgently.

The hands on the watch were beginning to quiver.

'Hang on! I have one more question!' Cindy's eyes were wide. She looked like she wanted to reach out and grab Leah, Mimi and George, but instead she curled her hands into her chest. 'Space. Do we . . . Does America ever make it?' She licked her lips nervously.

Leah smiled warmly. 'Oh yeah, loads of times,' she told her. She paused, and then added, 'Just you wait. An American astronaut will be the first person to set foot on the moon.'

Then, before it was too late, Leah clicked the watch crown twice.

Time slowed and everyone around the three of them froze. Leah took one last look at Cindy. Her eyes were saucers of surprise, her mouth open in a shout.

And then it was as if someone had taken a vacuum cleaner and sucked all of the colour out of the landscape, sending it spiralling round and round. Leah felt like she was in a washing machine as 1957 disintegrated and Langley, Virginia, vanished.

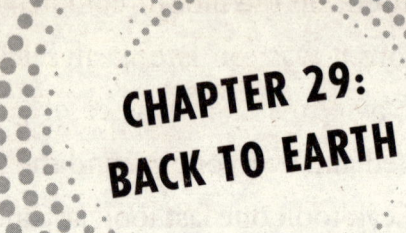

CHAPTER 29: BACK TO EARTH

Leah opened her eyes to the familiar sight of her bedroom.

She was on her bed, the duvet twisted and tangled beneath her. George and Mimi were both on the floor, their expressions dazed. Rolo pranced around them, barking enthusiastically. He jumped up at Mimi, plastering her face with soggy dog kisses.

'Ugh!' Mimi laughed, pushing him away. 'Thanks, Rolo. I missed you too!'

'Ahhh,' George sighed, closing his eyes and smiling. 'Thank goodness we're home!'

'I'm going to miss Cindy.' Mimi sighed. 'But I'm glad we managed to save Nancy.'

'And at least you didn't have to escape any

snakes this time, George,' Leah commented. 'Or fight off a leopard.' She swung her legs over the bed and tried to stand. A lance of pain shot through her knee and she stopped, hissing.

'What's up, L?' Mimi asked. 'Is it your knee?'

Leah rubbed at the blue bandage. 'Yeah,' she replied. 'It's really sore.'

'Well, we did have a pretty intense three days. There was a lot of running,' George said ruefully.

'I guess I'm just going to have to rest up.' Leah pushed herself back into her pillow, settling herself against the headboard.

'Do you think this will mean you'll have to take even more time off before you can come back to the football team?' Mimi asked, biting her lip.

Leah's shoulders sagged as she nodded. 'Probably.'

George frowned. 'You don't seem as upset about that as I thought you would be.'

It was true, Leah realized. She *didn't* feel as annoyed as she had before their trip back into the past. She was silent as she considered this.

'I think,' she said finally, 'that I learned something from Mr Whistler. He was selfish and he only looked after himself. He thought he needed to win the Space Race as quickly as he possibly could so that he could keep his job. It didn't matter if he wasn't doing that job properly or if people got hurt.' She took a deep breath. 'I don't want to be like that. If I don't do what the doctor says and take my time, my knee might not heal properly, and that'll mean I'll *never* get back on the football pitch. I'll be letting myself *and* the team down.'

Mimi smiled. 'Well, I guess I'll just have to try to hold everyone together until you're ready to come back!'

Leah laughed.

'Hey, do you think Cindy ever reached her goal?' George said. 'Do you think she ever became an engineer?'

'Let's see! Mimi, pass me my phone.' Mimi handed it over and Leah tapped the screen, entering her password and opening up a browser. In the search bar, she typed 'Cindy Grant'. The page filled with results, but it didn't take Leah long to find what she was looking for.

'Here she is!' she said excitedly. George and Mimi jumped onto the bed alongside her, clustering around the screen. Not wanting to be left out, Rolo hopped up too, settling himself in Leah's lap.

'*Cindy Grant was the first Black female engineer to work at NASA,*' Mimi read, her voice hitching with happiness. '*Despite many protests about her gender and the suitability of women working in the engineering industry, Cindy completed her exams and became one of the most respected engineers at NASA, working on the space programme until she retired. Her mother was the famous Nancy Grant. Nancy began her career as a human computer in the early fifties, when NASA was known as the NACA, but went on to work on the Apollo missions, helping to launch the first American – Alan Shepard – into space.*'

'*Now aged seventy-nine and retired, Cindy lives in Florida, close to Cape Canaveral,*' George continued, reading further down the page, '*so that she can watch the rockets whenever she wants to.*'

'She really did it,' Leah beamed. 'The first Black female engineer at NASA.'

'That's so cool,' George whispered.

Leah ran her fingers over Rolo's soft fur. She could only imagine how hard it must have been for Cindy to achieve her dream, especially when there had been so many people at the NACA who were determined to stop women from reaching their true potential. But their friend had never given up. She'd been patient and worked hard, knowing that one day she'd make it.

CHAPTER 30: ONE SMALL STEP

Leah danced from foot to foot, marking her opponent as the ball sped down the pitch towards them. He tried to break free to intercept the pass, but Leah was faster than him, and she sprang forward, sticking to his side like glue. He glared at her in frustration.

Opposite her, Ayo gave her a thumbs up and Leah grinned, her heart pumping in her chest. Adrenaline flooded her body and it felt wonderful. It had been so long since she'd had a chance to move her body like this. She'd missed it.

This match was Leah's first one back. After the watch had sent them home from Virginia, the doctor had recommended that Leah take four weeks out to rest. She'd been disappointed that it was such a long time, but she hadn't complained. Instead, she'd poured all of her energy into the exercises the doctor had given her. They were designed to help her knee grow stronger so that she could avoid getting the same type of injury again.

Now Leah watched as William tackled his opponent and stole the ball. He looked around for someone to pass it to, and Leah sped forwards, her arms and legs pumping. William kicked the ball towards her. She caught it easily on the inside of her foot and began to run with it towards the opposite goal. Behind her, there was a yelp of alarm as the other team tried to chase her.

'Here, L, here!' Mimi cried, and Leah's head shot up. Her friend had managed to get away from the defender that had been marking her. Leah swung her foot back and booted the ball towards her. As she did so, she felt a slight twinge in her knee and gave a little gasp, reaching down to rub it.

Mimi turned the ball towards the goal, the defenders were zooming towards her, but as always, Mimi was faster than them. She kicked the ball as hard as she could.

It soared into the top-left corner.

The team went wild, running towards her with their arms raised, pumping their fists into the air. On the sidelines, the crowd cheered and there were a series of flashes as George snapped photographs for the school newspaper.

Leah grinned happily, but instead of going to celebrate with her friends, she jogged gently over to the bench.

Miss Kaur frowned as she approached. 'Leah, everything okay?'

'Actually, miss,' Leah said. 'I think maybe I need to come off.'

Miss Kaur's eyebrows shot up. 'Really? What's wrong?' She tugged on the whistle hanging round her neck.

'It's just that my knee's starting to ache a bit,' Leah admitted. 'It's not too bad yet, but I don't want to stay out there and risk making it worse.'

'If you think it's time . . .' Miss Kaur said.

Leah nodded. 'This is only my first game back.

I want to take it slowly, so that I recover properly.'

Miss Kaur gave her an approving smile. 'I have to say, I'm impressed,' the coach told her. 'You're being very sensible about this whole situation.'

Leah shrugged. 'I've learned recently that it's a

bad idea to rush things. They never turn out how you hope they're going to.'

The coach told her to sit on the bench, and then she blew the whistle, beckoning the referee over. One of the subs started warming up, ready to take her place. On the pitch, William, Mimi and Ayo shot Leah a look of concern, but she smiled at them reassuringly.

She settled herself down, rubbing at her knee. Once upon a time, she would have hated being forced to come off early because of an injury, but now Leah only thought of Cindy and Nancy. Good things took time and being patient made them worth the wait. After all, the journey was just as important as reaching the goal. And sometimes, if the journey felt long and hard, it only made reaching the goal that bit sweeter. Well, Leah wasn't scared of a little waiting, especially because now she knew that taking her time and working hard would always get her to where she wanted to go. Football wasn't going anywhere, and neither was she.

THE INSPIRATION BEHIND THE STORIES AND CHARACTERS IN THE *WONDER TEAM AND THE SPACE RACE*

The Space Race was a real event that took place from the early 1950s to the mid-1970s. It was a competition between the United States of America and the Soviet Union (also known as the USSR) to see who could rule the stars. There was no clear winner: the Soviet Union launched the first person into space in 1961 (Yuri Gagarin), but the United States was the first to send people to the moon in 1969 (Neil Armstrong and Buzz Aldrin). The first woman to make it to space was Valentina Tereshkova, a Soviet cosmonaut, in 1963. The United States didn't match this until twenty years later when, in 1983, Sally Ride was launched into space in the Shuttle *Challenger*.

The Intrepid One and Two weren't real rockets, but there were plenty of other shuttles that were launched into space during the three decades in which the Space Race took place. Take a look at the timeline below to see some of the defining events that made up this incredible period in history.

1955 The Space Race begins! The USA and the USSR both announce their intention to send satellites into space.

4 October 1957 The USSR successfully launches Sputnik 1, the first satellite to orbit Earth.

3 November 1957 The USSR launches Sputnik 2, which carries a dog named Laika.

31 January 1958 The USA finally launches its own satellite into orbit: Explorer 1.

1 October 1958 The NACA (National Advisory Committee for Aeronautics) officially becomes NASA (the National Aeronautics and Space Administration).

12 September 1959 The USSR sends the first spacecraft to the moon: Luna 2.

31 January 1961 The USA sends a chimpanzee called Ham into space, and he survives the trip, returning home unharmed.

12 April 1961 The Russian cosmonaut Yuri Gagarin becomes the first man to complete a single orbit around the Earth in his spacecraft Vostok 1. This is a major victory for the USSR.

5 May 1961 Hot on Gagarin's heels, Alan

Shepard becomes the first American man in space, flying in Freedom 7.

16 June 1963 The first female into space is Valentina Tereshkova, a Russian woman who orbited the Earth forty-eight times in her spacecraft, Vostok 6.

18 March 1965 USSR cosmonaut Alexei Leonov carries out the first spacewalk, leaving his spacecraft for twelve minutes.

21 December 1968 The USA sends the first manned spacecraft to the moon: Apollo 8.

20 July 1969 Americans Neil Armstrong and Buzz Aldrin become the first people to step foot on the moon, as part of the Apollo 11 mission.

19 April 1971 The USSR launches the first space station into orbit.

31 July 1971 The American David Scott becomes the first person to drive on the moon.

17 July 1975 Tom Stafford, an American, and Alexei Leonov, a Russian, exchange the first handshake in space, signalling the end of the Space Race. From this point on, the USA and the USSR work together to advance space exploration.

Langley, Virginia, USA, is a real place, and so were all the human 'computers' that worked there running calculations to help launch rockets into space. Nancy Grant and her daughter Cindy didn't exist, but there were many incredible women who inspired their creation.

Katherine Johnson
Katherine Johnson was an African American mathematician who worked in the West Computing Area as a human computer. Her job was to calculate and analyse the flight paths of spacecraft. The work she did was key to launching the first American man into space and, eventually, sending astronauts to the moon. She worked at NASA for three decades and retired in 1986.

Mary Jackson
Like Katherine Johnson, Mary Jackson was a human computer in the West Computing Area, though she didn't stay there long. Jackson had a passion for maths and science, and she wanted to become an engineer – just like Cindy. At this

time, the engineering training programmes were only open to white people, so Jackson had to get special permission to attend. Although in our story, Cindy became the first Black female engineer, in real life, this accolade belongs to Mary Jackson, who earned the position when the NACA became NASA in 1958. She continued to work there for the next twenty-seven years, until she retired in 1985.

Dorothy Vaughan

Dorothy Vaughan was also a human computer in the West Computing group and was the first African American manager at the NACA. When the NACA became NASA, the space programme began to use real computers rather than humans to run the mathematical calculations. Vaughan learned FORTRAN, the computer programming language these machines used, and oversaw these operations. She retired in 1971.

The Mercury Thirteen

The Mercury Thirteen were the inspiration for

the Venus Eleven, the fictional group of female astronauts that Miss Sinclair belonged to. In real life, between 1960 and 1961, thirteen American women underwent testing to see if they would be suitable astronaut candidates. They performed very well, and on some tests they even outperformed the men! Despite this, however, the programme wasn't supported by NASA, and it was later cancelled.

After this, NASA made it very difficult for women to become astronauts at all, stating that they needed to be graduates of military jet test pilot schools. Women were forbidden from entering these schools, so were unable to meet the requirements. An American woman didn't make it into space until Sally Ride flew on the Space Shuttle *Challenger* in 1983.

Rosa Parks
Rosa Parks was neither an astronaut nor an engineer, but she played a vital role in the American Civil Rights Movement. This was an important campaign designed to give Black

Americans the same rights as white citizens, and it took place between 1954 and 1968.

A crucial part of this struggle was the Montgomery Bus Boycott. In 1955, buses in Montgomery, Alabama, were segregated, which meant Black and white people couldn't sit together. However, one day, on a busy bus, Rosa Parks refused to give her seat up for a white passenger and she was arrested. As a result, civil rights supporters across Montgomery refused to use the buses until, in 1956, the Supreme Court dissolved Montgomery's segregation laws, finally allowing Black and white Americans to sit wherever they wanted.

A Note About 1957

Although we've done our best to be as historically accurate as possible when describing 1950s America and the events that took place during this decade, there have been a few instances where we've had to bend the truth to fit the story and make it easier for our heroes to save the day. We'd just like to take this opportunity to point out anything we've changed in the name of creativity.

Firstly, the launch of *Sputnik 2* happened on 3 November, 1957; however, this was actually a Sunday. So that Leah and her friends didn't have to go to work on the weekend, we've amended this, staging the launch on a Thursday, instead.

We've also taken some creative liberties with how advanced computers were at this time. In the control room at the NACA, for example, computers as we understand them today wouldn't have existed, and nor would computer hacking, either. In reality, the first computers that were used at the NACA were those operated by the likes of Dorothy Vaughan, designed purely to carry out complex mathematical calculations.

ABOUT THE AUTHORS

Leah Williamson plays as a defender for Arsenal and the Lionesses, England Women's Football team. In the summer of 2022, Leah captained the Lionesses to victory in the UEFA Women's Euro 2022.

As the first captain in the men's or women's senior teams to lead England to a European victory, Leah is uniquely positioned to motivate and inspire younger generations, and her first book, *You Have the Power*, is an empowering guide for children.

Jordan Glover book and as an adult, not much has changed. After completing her history degree at The University of Edinburgh in 2014, Jordan trained as a teacher and taught Key Stage 2 before becoming a full-time writer. She now holds a Master's degree with Distinction in Creative Writing from the Open University.

When not searching for magic and adventure

between the pages of her current read, you can find Jordan living in Cambridgeshire, embarking on thrilling escapades with her husband, son, cat, and dog. *The Wonder Team and the Space Race* is the fourth instalment in the bestselling The Wonder Team series.

ABOUT THE ILLUSTRATOR

Robin Boyden is a freelance illustrator based in Herefordshire in the West of England. In 2007, he graduated from University College Falmouth with a First Class Honours degree and soon after completed a Master's in Art and Design.

Robin works in the picture book and middle-grade fiction market and has previously worked as an editorial illustrator. He has twice been selected for the AOI Images annual and has worked for numerous clients in the publishing and editorial sectors worldwide.

ACKNOWLEDGEMENTS

From Leah

We are blessed to be able to continue this journey whilst fully supported by the people around us! Thank you to Macmillan for their continuing love for this series. Jordan, you're incredible.

From Jordan

As usual, there are far too many thank-yous to fit into such a small space but I'll do my best.

Firstly, thank you to my cousin, Leah. I can't believe we're still on this crazy rollercoaster together! Let's never get off.

Thank you also to everyone at Tongue-Tied Media and Macmillan who work so hard to bring these books to life. We'd be a mess without you!

As always, thanks to my writing gals, who keep me going when putting words down on paper just feels too hard.

Thank you to Tim, who valiantly attempted to

teach me rocket science over WhatsApp. I know it wasn't easy!

A massive thank you to my family, especially Rob and Henry. You're my biggest cheerleaders and I love you eternally.

And, lastly, a massive thanks to you, the readers, who continue to support us and buy these books. Without you, we wouldn't be able to create the stories that we do.

JOIN THE WONDER TEAM ON MORE TIME-TWISTING ADVENTURES!